Undead and Uneasy

Berkley Sensation titles by MaryJanice Davidson

UNDEAD AND UNWED
UNDEAD AND UNEMPLOYED
UNDEAD AND UNAPPRECIATED
UNDEAD AND UNRETURNABLE
UNDEAD AND UNPOPULAR
UNDEAD AND UNEASY

DEAD AND LOVING IT

DERIK'S BANE

Undead and Uneasy

MaryJanice Davidson

BERKLEY SENSATION, NEW YORK

THE BERKLEY PUBLISHING GROUP
Published by the Penguin Group
Penguin Group (USA) Inc.
375 Hudson Street, New York, New York 10014, USA
Penguin Group (Canada), 90 Eglinton Avenue East, Suite 700, Toronto, Ontario M4P 2Y3, Canada
(a division of Pearson Penguin Canada Inc.)
Penguin Books Ltd., 80 Strand, London WC2R 0RL, England
Penguin Group Ireland, 25 St. Stephen's Green, Dublin 2, Ireland (a division of Penguin Books Ltd.)
Penguin Group (Australia), 250 Camberwell Road, Camberwell, Victoria 3124, Australia
(a division of Pearson Australia Group Pty. Ltd.)
Penguin Books India Pvt. Ltd., 11 Community Centre, Panchsheel Park, New Delhi—110 017, India
Penguin Group (NZ), 67 Apollo Drive, Rosedale, North Shore 0745, Auckland, New Zealand
(a division of Pearson New Zealand Ltd.)
Penguin Books (South Africa) (Pty.) Ltd., 24 Sturdee Avenue, Rosebank, Johannesburg 2196,
South Africa

Penguin Books Ltd., Registered Offices: 80 Strand, London WC2R 0RL, England

This book is an original publication of The Berkley Publishing Group.

This is a work of fiction. Names, characters, places, and incidents either are the product of the author's imagination or are used fictitiously, and any resemblance to actual persons, living or dead, business establishments, events, or locales is entirely coincidental. The publisher does not have any control over and does not assume any responsibility for author or third-party websites or their content.

Copyright © 2007 by MaryJanice Alongi
Text design by Kristin del Rosario

First edition: June 2007

Library of Congress Cataloging-in-Publication Data

Davidson, MaryJanice.
    Undead and uneasy / MaryJanice Davidson.
        p.   cm.
    ISBN 978-0-425-21376-6
 1. Vampires—Fiction.   I. Title.

    PS3604.A949U5253 2007
    813'.6—dc22

                                                                    2007005973

PRINTED IN THE UNITED STATES OF AMERICA

10   9   8   7   6   5   4   3   2   1

Thanks to my long-suffering husband (fourteen years of marriage by the time you hold this book in your hand, poor bastard . . . my husband, not you), my supportive family, Jessica, and my readers . . . long may your credit cards reign.

Acknowledgments

This book was written alone, but several of the usual suspects helped, either by making suggestions or telling me to get my big butt back into the office chair. In no particular order, they are: Tony; Chris; Liam; Yvonne; Mom; and my Dad, the artist formerly known as King Al (see *The Royal Treatment*; *The Royal Surprise*).

But it's also dedicated to friends I've never met. All the members of my Yahoo group, for one. This is the nicest group on the Internet, sharing pictures, stories, and best of all, book recommendations. I also post new chapter excerpts and drop annoying hints about upcoming books and plot developments to the Yahoos. If you'd like to join, you can check it out at maryjanice-subscribe@yahoogroups.com. Special thanks to Terri, Mippy, and Jose, who always put a smile on my face.

Another ridiculously supportive group is the Laurell K. Hamilton forum (www.laurellkhamilton.org). I mean, these aren't even her books, this is *her* website to promote her work, and not only does she make room for a Web page of mine, but everyone there is super nice: they support me, buy my books, discuss same, meet me at book signings, and ask for autographs. Weird. But nice.

Frankly, the romance world is full of warm, supporting authors. Among the best of the best: Charlaine Harris, Susan Grant, P. C. Cast, Nora Roberts, Lori Foster, and Christine Feehan.

I write the books, but no book can get on the shelves, or stay on the shelves, without phenomenal PR representation. In this I am blessed with Julia Fleischaker of Berkley PR and Jessica Growette of J.A.G. Promotions. Their job sucks, because they do the hard work and I get all the glory.

Speaking of sucky, horrible jobs with no glory (no, Mom, I'm not talking about you), there's my editor, Cindy Hwang, and my agent, Ethan Ellenberg. Both have had more than their fair share of migraines, thanks to yours truly.

But this book, and all the ones before it, would not have been possible without e-publishers and e-books. They took a chance on this writer when no one knew me, and I appreciate it.

This past summer I went on my first book tour, which was harrowing yet thrilling. And a lot of the things you're about to read in this book were directly inspired by questions and comments readers asked me at signings and readings. So thanks for caring enough to show up, for caring about characters enough to be concerned about them, and finally, thanks to David, who cornered me (in the very nicest way) at a book signing and begged me to get Marc Spangler hooked up. He was not alone in this request and I, the obedient author, obeyed.

Also, thanks to Martha Stewart, whose Wedding DVD was a great help in figuring out what Betsy's gown, cake, and bridesmaids' dresses would look like.

Thanks to Jamie Poole for thinking up The Betsy, a delightful cocktail that lubricated my creativity on more than one occasion. Take that however you like.

And finally, a tip of the hat to my readers, especially those of you who've been at this since the original *Undead and Unwed*. This is a book that goes where the first five really haven't. That's not to say we won't have fun along the way . . . those of you who've been with me before know this universe is always a good time.

And the Queene shalt noe a living childe, and he shalt be hers by a living man.

—THE BOOK OF THE DEAD

A cat's a better mother than you.

—MARGARET MITCHELL, *Gone With the Wind*

A gloomy guest fits not a wedding feast.

—FRIEDRICH VON SCHILLER

Lisa, vampires *are* make believe. Like elves, gremlins, and Eskimos.

—THE SIMPSONS, "Treehouse of Horror IV"

With enough courage, you can do without a reputation. —MARGARET MITCHELL, *Gone With the Wind*

To challenge the Queene, thou shalt desecrate the symbole. —THE BOOK OF THE DEAD

Crying is all right in its own way while it lasts. But you have to stop sooner or later, and then you still have to decide what to do. —C. S. LEWIS, *The Silver Chair*

A Letter to My Readers

First of all, thank you, dear reader. It's standard to refer to you as "dear" but you really are dear to me, and I'll tell you why. Thanks to you, I've gone from the excitement of never knowing when the power will be shut off (during a party? when my folks are over? during my kid's science experiment?) to the staid, dull lifestyle of one who can actually pay her utility bills. Because of my readers, I never go to a book signing unless I'm sporting (a) designer shoes or (b) a pedicure. Because of my readers, I've gotten to research mermaids, ghosts, psychics, manta rays, the Caymans, Florida, Cape Cod, Monterey Bay, Texas, zombies (Texas zombies?), vampires, were-anythings, Alaska, royal lineage, Martha Stewart, bellinis vs. mimosas, bed and breakfasts, wax fangs, and why nobody starts smoking at age thirty-five.

I've also learned how to write an ongoing series versus a stand-alone single-title novel.

Which brings us to *Undead and Uneasy*.

If you've been with me since the beginning, since *Undead and Unwed*, bless you. Your patience is about to be rewarded, I think. If you're new to the series, you've come along just in time: as one of the weird sisters in *Hercules* said, "It's gonna be big."

Everything in the Undead universe has been leading to this book (say it with me: poor Betsy!). Yes, there has been a method to my madness. The support group she has so carefully, if unconsciously, been building around herself, that I've been building for her, is about to disappear. Everything she thought she knew about the undead? Totally wrong. Marriage? Life? Death? It's all, like her favorite book and movie, *Gone With the Wind*.

That's not to say we won't have some fun along the way . . . those of you who've been with me before know that the Undead universe is always a good time. It's just . . . we're not all going to make it out alive. And I'm sorry. I know that sucks. But it's just . . . it's just how life is sometimes. And death.

So, dear reader, thank you for coming along for the ride. Thank you for *staying* along for the ride. You won't be sorry, I'm pretty sure. And if you are? Well, I can write fast or I can write long, but I can't do both. This is the long version, so what say we give it a try?

So let's get going, shall we? As Betsy might say, "Pipe down and listen up, asshat."

You are cordially invited to
the wedding of

Elizabeth Anne Taylor

and

Sinclair

607 Summit Avenue
Midnight
July 4, 2007

RSVP by June 25, and don't be one of those jerks
who doesn't RSVP and then shows up with
three people. Seriously.

Prologue

Once, there was a beautiful queen who was as terrible on the inside as she was glorious on the outside. She was vain, wicked, cold, and selfish. Her greatest pleasures were her coalfire earrings, terrible wieldy things that swung past her shoulders. Each stone was as big around as the ball of the queen's thumb, and it was said more than a thousand men died mining the bloodred rocks.

So conceited was this queen, and so greatly did she love her coalfire earrings, that she threatened a curse upon any who might steal them from her. So naturally, her people waited until the queen died before taking them.

The four thieves (who in truth cannot be called grave robbers, because no one waited until the hated queen was buried) went to her unguarded body and helped themselves. The body was unguarded because the parties celebrating the new monarchs (the dead queen's cousin, a plain but generous woman; and her husband, a shy healer) were in full swing, and no one especially cared about guarding a dead jerk.

The first of the four dropped dead before he could mount his horse. The second of the four died after his tent mysteriously caught fire the next night. The third made it to the coast, sold the earrings for a splendid sum, and promptly dropped dead of a brainstorm, what today is known as an aneurysm. What happened to the fourth is not known.

The man who bought the earrings had them in his shop for three and a half days. He sold the earrings to a man of some wealth and standing, just before his shop was struck by hundreds of successive strokes of lightning, sparing his life but driving him out of business forever, and leaving him with a lifelong fear of flashing lights and loud noises.

The man of wealth and standing was the manservant of a European prince (history is vague on which one). He delivered the earrings to his master, and one hour later, the prince ingested a lethal amount of tainted meat, along with half of one of the earrings, which was later extracted during the autopsy.

The earrings eventually reached London, but not after causing a series of increasingly odd and gruesome disasters along the way, including but not limited to a pig plague, a tomato blight, a series of foals born with five legs, multiple drownings several miles away from any natural source of water, and a viciously quick mammal that no one ever saw clearly enough to describe well.

The day the jewelry went on display at the British Museum in their Return of Egyptian Antiquities Exhibit, the head of security suffered a fatal heart attack, the gift shop girl went blind, and three tour guides were stricken with crippling dysentery.

The earrings stayed in the museum for many years. Probably. The earrings, it seemed, disliked staying in one spot, and curators were known to snatch themselves bald looking for the jewels.

They turned up once in the Neanderthal exhibit,

twice in the men's urinal on the second floor, six times in the gift shop (by now word of the "cursed" earrings had spread, and no museum employee, no matter how long her hours or how low her pay, dared touch them), and four times in the cafeteria (where an unwary museum guest nearly choked to death on one). They also went on an unscheduled, miniature tour around the world, disappearing and being found in no fewer than eight exhibits: Japan, Rome, Manila, Greece, the Americas, Britain, the Pacific, and the Near East. Each of the other museums, aware of the artifacts' history, returned the jewels to Britain quickly and without comment.

Eventually the British Museum came under new management (the last curator having taken forced early retirement for mysteriously losing his fingers and his sense of smell) who, in an attempt to score points with the House of Windsor, made a gift of the earrings to Diana, the Princess of Wales.

Some time later, they came into the possession of a very old, very curious vampire who had the idea of breaking the earrings into a series of smaller stones and shipping them in twenty-five different directions around the planet. You know, just to see what would happen.

One of the stones ended up in Minnesota, right about at the turn of the twenty-first century. Nobody knows the exact date, because those involved in the shipment arrangements simply cannot be found.

Chapter 1

T here are three things wrong with that card," the king of the vampires told me. "One, my love for you is not anything like 'shimmering amber waves of summer wheat.' Two, my love for you has nothing to do with adorable, fluffy cartoon rabbits. Three . . ." And he sighed here. "Rabbits do not sparkle."

I looked at the shiny yellow card, aglitter with sparkling bunnies. It was the least objectionable of the pile of two dozen I had spread all over our bed. What could I say? He had a point. Three of them. "It's just an example—don't have a heart attack and friggin' die on me, all right?"

"I do not have," he muttered, "that kind of good fortune."

"I heard that. I'm just saying, there will be a lot of people at the wedding"—I ignored Sinclair's shudder—"but there will also be people who can't make it. You know, due to having other plans or being dead, or whatever. So what you do is, you send a wedding announcement to pull in all the people who couldn't come. That way people know we actually did the deed. It's polite." I racked my brain for the perfect way to describe it so my reluctant groom would clamber aboard. "It's, you know, civilized."

"It is a voracious grab for gifts from the crude and uncouth."

"That's true," I acknowledged after a minute, knowing well where I was in the Wars of the Couth. Come on, we all knew he was right. There was no point—*no* point—in all those birth and wedding and graduation announcements beyond, "Hey! Limber up the old checkbook; something new has happened in our family. Cash is also fine."

"But it's still nice. You didn't fuss nearly so much about the invitations."

"The invitations have a logical point."

"The invitations are weird. Just 'Sinclair,' like you don't have a middle or first name. Why wouldn't you put your full name on the thing?"

"Our community knows me as Sinclair."

'Our' my butt. He meant the vampire community. I couldn't resist one last dig. "I'm marrying Cher!"

"Don't tease."

I bit my tongue for what felt like the hundredth time that night . . . and it was barely 9:00 p.m. With the wedding only three weeks away, Sinclair, my blushing groom, was growing bitchier by the hour.

He had never liked the idea of a formal wedding with a minister and flower girls and a wedding cake frosted with colored Crisco. He said that because the Book of the Dead proclaimed him my consort, we were already married and would be for a thousand years. Period. End of discussion. Everything else? A waste of time. And money. Tough to tell the greater sin in his eyes.

After what seemed like a thousand years (but was only one and a half) I'd gotten Eric (yes, he had a first name) to profess his love, propose, give me a ring, and agree to a ceremony. But he never promised to take his dose without kicking, and he sure never promised to get married without a heavy dose of snark.

I had two choices. I could rise to his bitchy comments with a few of my own, and we could end up in a wicked big fight, again. Or, I could ignore his bitchy comments and go about my day, er, night, and after the wedding, Sinclair would be my sweet blushing boy-toy again.

Then there was the honeymoon to look forward to: two weeks in New York City, a place I'd never been! I'd heard NYC was a great place to visit, if you had money. Sinclair had gobs of money to his name. Ew, which reminded me.

"By the way, I'm not taking your name. It's nothing personal—"

"Not personal? It is my name."

"—it's just how I was raised."

"Your mother took your father's name and, even after he left her for the lethal flirtations of another woman, kept his name. Which is why, to this day, there are two Mrs. Taylors in town. So in fact, it is *not* how you were raised."

I glared. He glared back, except his was more like a sneer. Since Sinclair looked like he was sneering even when he was unconscious, it was tough to tell. All I knew was, we were headed for yet another argument and thank goodness we were doing it in our bedroom, where one of the house's many live-ins weren't likely to bother us. Or, even worse, rate us (Marc had given our last fight a 7.6—we started with an 8 based on volume alone, but he had taken four-tenths of a point off for lack of originality in name-calling).

We lived (and would presumably for the next thousand years—hope Jessica was paid up on her damage insurance) in a big old mansion on Summit Avenue in St. Paul. Me, Sinclair, my best friend Jessica, Marc, and a whole bunch of others I'm just too tired to list right now. I adored my friends, but sometimes I couldn't help wishing they'd all just disappear for the sake of some peace and quiet.

Retreating to the master suite, where we were currently arguing, was an acceptable substitute for actual solitude. I'd never seen a divine bathroom before, much less been in one, but after taking a bath in the eight-foot-long whirlpool tub, I'd come to believe God could act through bubbles.

The whole place was like a bed and breakfast—the fanciest, nicest one in the whole world, where the fridge was always full, the sheets were always fresh, and you never had to check out and go home. Even the closets were sublime, with more scrollwork than you could shake a stick at. Having come from a long line of tract housing families, I'd resisted the move here last year. But now I loved it. I still couldn't believe I actually lived in a *mansion* of all things. Some of the rooms were so big, I hardly noticed Sinclair.

Okay, that was a lie. Eric Sinclair filled every room he was in, even if he was just sitting in the corner reading a newspaper. Big—well over six feet—with the build of a farmer (which he had been) who kept in shape (which he did): wide, heavily muscled shoulders, long legs, narrow waist, flat stomach, big hands, big teeth, big dick. Alpha male all the way. And he was mine. Mine, I tell you!

Sinclair was seventy-something—I was vague on the details, and he rarely volunteered autobiographical info—but had died in his thirties, so his black hair was unmarked by gray; his broad, handsome face was without so much as a sun wrinkle. He had a grin that made Tom Cruise look like a snaggle-toothed octogenarian.

He was dynamite in bed—ooh, boy, was he! He was rich (possibly richer than Jessica, who had arranged for the purchase of this mansion). He was strong—I'd seen him pull a man's arm off his body like you or I would pull a chicken wing apart. And I mentioned the vampire part, right? That he was the king of the vampires?

And I was the queen. *His* queen.

Never mind what the Book of the Dead said, never mind that he'd tricked me into the queen gig, never mind what other vampires said; shit, never mind what my *mom* said. I loved Eric (when he wasn't being a pud), and he loved me (I was almost positive); and in my book (which wasn't bound in human skin and written in blood, *thank you very much*) that meant we collared a justice of the peace and got him to say "Husband and Wife."

Two years ago, I would have said a minister. But if a man of God said a blessing over Eric Sinclair, sprinkled him with holy water, or handed him a collection plate, my darling groom would go up in flames, and it'd be really awkward.

Anyway, that was the way I wanted things. The way I needed them. And really, it seemed a small enough thing to ask. Especially when you look at all the shit *I* had put up with since rising from the dead. Frankly, if the king of the vampires didn't like it, he could take a flying fuck at a rolling garter belt.

"If you don't like it," I said, "you can take a flying fuck at a rolling garter belt."

"Is that another of your tribe's charming post-ceremony activities?"

"What is this 'my tribe' crapola?" I'd given up on the announcements and had started folding my T-shirts—the basket had been silently condemning me for almost a week. Jessica had hired plenty of servants, but we all insisted on doing our own laundry. Except Sinclair. I think Tina (his super-butler/major domo/assistant) did his. He could hold his damned breath waiting for *me* to step up.

I dropped the fresh, clean T-shirt so I could put my hands on my hips and *really* give him the glare. "Your dad was a Minnesota farmer. This I'm-an-aristocrat-and-you're-a-peasant schtick stinks like a rotten apple."

Sinclair, working at the desk in the corner (in a black suit, on a Tuesday night—it was the equivalent of a guy getting up on his day off and immediately putting on a Kenneth Cole before so much as eating a bowl of cornflakes), simply shrugged and did not look up. That was his way: to taunt, to make an irritating observation, and then refuse to engage. He swore it was proof of his love, that he'd have killed anyone else months ago.

"I am just so sick of you acting like this wedding thing is all me and has nothing to do with you."

He didn't look up, and he didn't put his pen down. "This wedding thing *is* all you and has nothing to do with me."

"I'll bet you haven't even worked on your vows yet."

"I certainly have."

"Fine, smart-ass. Let's hear it."

He laid his pen down, closed his eyes, licked his lips, and took a deep breath. "Alas, the penis is such a ridiculous petitioner. It is so unreliable, though everything depends on it—the world is balanced on it like a ball on a seal's nose. It is so easily teased, insulted, betrayed, abandoned; yet it must pretend to be invulnerable, a weapon which confers magical powers upon its possessor; consequently this muscle-less inchworm must try to swagger through temples and pull apart thighs like the hairiest Samson, the mightiest ram." Opening his eyes and taking in my horrified expression, he added, "William Gass, 'Metaphor and Measurement'."

Then he picked up his pen and returned to his work.

With a shriek of rage, I yanked my engagement ring off my finger, yelped (it stuck to my second knuckle), and threw it at him, hard.

He snatched it out of the air without looking and tossed it back at me. I flailed at it, juggled it madly, then finally clenched it in my cold fist.

"Oh no you don't, love. You insisted on a gauche representation of my feelings and you *will* wear it. And if you throw it at me again," he continued absently, turning crumbling sheets of parchments, never looking up, "I will make you eat it."

"Eat *this*." I flipped him the bird. I could actually feel my blood pressure climbing. Not that I had blood pressure. But I knew what it felt like. And I knew I was acting like a brat. But what was the matter with him? Why was he being so cold, so distant, so—so Sinclair? We hadn't even made love since . . . I started counting on my fingers and gave up after I'd reached last Thursday. Instead we were sharing blood without sex—a first for us. It was like—like being used like a Kleenex and tossed accordingly.

What was wrong with him? What was wrong with me? I was getting everything I ever wanted. Since I woke up dead, right? *Right?*

I was so caught up in my mental bitching I hadn't noticed that Sinclair had advanced on me like a cat on a rat.

"Put your trinket on, darling, lest you lose it again."

I ignored the urge to pierce his left nostril with it. He was *soooo* lucky I liked rubies.

I managed (barely) to evade his kiss. "What? You think we're going to have sex now?"

"I had hopes," he admitted, dodging a fist.

"Don't we have to make up before the makeup sex?"

"I don't see why," he said, pressing me down onto the bed.

I grumbled, but his hands felt fine, and I figured it was just as well to let him think he was in charge. (He did only *think* that, right?) His mouth was on mine, then on my neck, his hands were under my shirt, then tugging and pulling on my pants. I felt his teeth pierce my throat, felt the dizzying sensation of being taken, being used, as he sipped my cool blood. His hands were on my ass, pulling me toward him, and then he was sliding into me, and that was that, the fight was over. Or at least on hold.

We rocked together for a fine time, and I counted my orgasms like fireworks going off in my brain: one, two, three!

(Elizabeth, my own, my queen, my . . . bride.)

"Get used to that one," I panted, meeting his thrusts with my hips, trying not to hear the laughter in his head.

He bit me on the other side of my throat, and I thought, we're going to have to change the sheets. Stupid undead lovemaking!

He stiffened over me and then rolled away, stifling a yawn. "There, now. Don't you feel better?"

"Loads. So about the wedding—"

"The ceremony we have no use for?"

Poof. All gone, afterglow. "Shut *up*! Some moldy old book written by dead guys tells you we're married, and that's good enough for you?"

"Are we discussing the Book of the Dead, or the"— He made a terrible face, like he was trying to spit out a mouse, and then coughed it out—"Bible?"

"Very funny!" Though I was impressed; even a year ago, he could never have said Bible. Maybe I was rubbing off on him? He was certainly rubbing off on me; I'd since found out the *Wall Street Journal* made splendid kindling. "Look, I'd just like you to say, just once, just this one time, I'd like to hear that you're happy we're getting married."

"I am happy," he yawned, "and we *are* married."

And around and around we went. I wasn't stupid. I was aware that to the vampires, the Book of the Dead *was* a bible of sorts, and if it said we were consorts and coregents, then it was a done deal.

But I was a different sort of vampire. I'd managed (I think) to hang on to my humanity. A little, anyway. And I wanted a real wedding. With cake, even if I couldn't eat it. And flowers. And Sinclair slipping a ring on my finger and looking at me like I was the only woman in the universe for him. A ring to match the gorgeous gold engagement band clustered with diamonds and rubies, wholly unique and utterly beautiful and *proof that I was his*. And me looking understated yet devastating in a smashingly simple wedding gown, looking scrumptious and gorgeous for him. Looking *bridal*. And him looking dark and sinister and frightening to everyone except me. Him *smiling* at me, not that nasty-nice grin he used on everyone else.

And we'd be a normal couple. A nice, normal couple who could start a—start a—

"I just wish we could have a baby," I fretted, twisting my ring around and around on my finger.

"We have been over this before," he said with barely concealed distaste.

We had. Or I had. Don't get me wrong; I wasn't one of those whiny women (on the subject of drooling infants, anyway), but it was like once I knew I could never have one (and once my rotten stepmother, the Ant, *did* have one), it was all I could think about.

No baby for Betsy and Sinclair. Not ever. I'd even tried to adopt a ghost once, but once I fixed her problem, she vanished, and that was that. I had no plans to put my heart on the chopping block again.

I sat up in bed much too fast, slipped, and hit the floor with a thud. "Don't you want a baby, Sinclair?"

"We have been over this before," he repeated, still not looking at me. "The Book of the Dead says the Queen can have a child with a living man."

"Fuck the Book of the Dead! I want our baby, Sinclair, yours and mine!"

"I cannot give you one," he said quietly, and left

me to go back to his desk. He sat down, squinted at some paperwork, and was immediately engrossed.

Right. He couldn't. He was dead. We could never be real parents. Which is why I wanted (stop me if you've heard this before) *a real wedding*. With flowers and booze and cake and dresses and tuxes.

And my family and friends looking at us and thinking, *now there's a couple that will make it, there's a couple that was meant to be*. And Marc having a date, and Jessica not being sick anymore. And my baby brother not crying once, and my stepmother getting along with everybody and not looking tacky.

And our other roommate werewolf, Antonia, not having a million bitchy remarks about "monkey rituals" and George the Fiend—I mean Garrett—not showing us how he can eat with his feet. And Cathie not whispering in my ear and making me giggle at inappropriate moments.

And my folks not fighting, and peace being declared in the Middle East just before the fireworks (and doves) went up in the backyard, and someone discovering that chocolate cured cancer.

Was that so much to ask?

Chapter 2

ake that rag off," my best friend rasped. "It makes you look like a dead crack whore."

"Not a *dead* one," my roommate, Marc, mock-gasped. "How positively blech-o."

"It's not that bad," I said doubtfully, twirling before the mirror. But Jess was right. Nordic pale when alive, I was positively ghastly when dead, and a pure white gown made me look like—it must be said—a corpse bride.

"I think it looks very pretty," Laura, my half sister, said loyally. Of course, Laura thought everything was very pretty. *Laura* was very pretty. She was also the devil's daughter, but that was a story for another time.

The five of us—Marc, Jessica, Laura, Cathie, and I—were at Rush's Bridal, an überexclusive bridal shop that had been around for years, that you could only get in by appointment, that had provided Mrs. Hubert Humphrey and her bridesmaids with their gowns. (The thank you note was framed in the shop.)

Thanks to Jessica's pull, I hadn't needed an appointment. But I didn't like stores like this. It wasn't like a Macy's . . . you couldn't go back in the racks and browse. You told the attendant what you wanted, and they fetched (arf!) various costly gowns for you to try on.

I found this frustrating, because I didn't *know* what I wanted. Sure, I'd been flipping through *Minnesota Bride* since seventh grade, but that was when I had a rosy complexion. And a pulse. And no money. But all that had changed.

"I'm sure we'll find something just perfect for you," the attendant, whose name I kept forgetting, purred, as she had me strip to my paisley panties. I didn't care. Jessica had seen me naked about a zillion times (once, naked and crying in a closet), Laura was family, and Marc was gay. Oh, and Cathie was dead. Deader than me, even. A ghost.

"So how's the blushing bridegroom?" Marc asked, surreptitiously trying to take Jessica's pulse. She slapped him away like she would an annoying wasp.

"Grumpy," I said, as more attendants with armfuls of tulle appeared. "I swear. I was completely prepared to become Bridezilla—"

"We were, too," Cathie muttered.

"—but nobody warned me Sinclair would get all bitchy."

"Not pure white," Jessica said tiredly. "It washes her out. How about an Alexia with black trim?"

"No black," I said firmly. "At a vampire wedding? Are you low on your meds?"

Marc frowned. "Actually, yes."

"Never mind," I sighed. "There's lots of shades of white. Cream, latte, ecru, ivory, magnolia, seashell—"

"You don't have to wear white," Laura piped up, curled up like a cat in a velvet armchair. Her sunny blond hair was pulled back in a severe bun. She was dressed in a sloppy blue T-shirt and cutoffs. Bare legs, flip-flops. She still looked better than I was going to look on The Day, and it was taking all my willpower not to locate a shotgun from somewhere in that bridal shop's secret back room and shoot her in the head. Not to kill her, of course. Just to make her face slightly less symmetrical. "In fact, it's inappropriate for you to wear white."

"Virgin," I sneered.

"Vampire," Laura retorted. "You could wear blue. Or red! Red would bring out your eyes."

"Stop! You're all killing me with your weirdness."

"What's the budget on this thing, anyway?" Cathie asked, drifting close to the ceiling, inspecting the chandeliers, the gorgeous accessories, the beautifully dressed yet understated attendants (who were ignoring all the vampire talk, as good attendants did), the utter lack of a price tag on anything.

"Mmmm mmmm," I muttered.

"What?" Cathie and Jessica asked in unison.

"Cathie was just asking about the budget." One of the yuckier perks of being queen of the dead? I alone could see and hear ghosts. And they could see and hear me. And bug me. Any time. Day or night. Naked or fully clothed.

But even for a ghost, Cathie was special. As we all

know, most ghosts hang around because they have un-
finished business. Once they finished their business,
poof! Off into the wild blue whatever. (God knows
I'd never had that privilege.) And who could blame
them? If it were me, I'd beat feet off this mortal plane
the minute I could.

But even after I'd fixed Cathie's little serial killer
problem, she hung around. She even ran defense between the ghosts and me. Sort of like a celestial exec-
utive assistant.

"So?" Marc asked.

"Don't look at . . . me," Jessica gasped. Marc's lips
thinned, and we all looked away. "Gravy train's . . .
over."

"Would your friend like some water?" a new attendant said, swooping in out of nowhere.

"Got any chemo?" Jess asked tiredly.

"It's, um, three million," I said, desperate to change
the subject. I couldn't look at Jessica, so I looked at my
feet instead. My toenails were in dire need of filing
and polishing. As they always were—no matter what I
did to them, they always returned to the same state
they'd been in the night I died.

"Three *million*?" Cathie screamed in my ear, making me flinch. The attendants probably thought I was epileptic. "What, rubles? Pesos? Yen?"

"Three million *dollars*?" Marc goggled. "For a party?"

All the women glared at him. Men! A wedding wasn't 'just a party.' A *party* was 'just a party.' This would be the most important day of my—our—lives.

Still. I was sort of amazed to find Sinclair had dumped three mill into my checking account. I didn't even bother asking him how he'd pulled it off.

"What the *hell* will you spend three million on?" Cathie shrieked.

"Cake, of course."

"Talking to Cathie?" Laura asked.

"Yeah. Cake—" I continued.

"Cathie, you should go to your king," Laura suggested.

"King?" Cathie asked in my head.

"She means Jesus," I said.

"This haunting isn't very becoming," my sister continued doggedly.

"Tell your goody-goody sister to cram it," Cathie said.

"She says thanks for the advice," I said.

"Just think of all the charitable contributions you could make with that money," Laura gently chided me, "and still have a perfectly lovely ceremony." (Have I mentioned that the devil's daughter was raised by ministers?)

"There's the cake," I continued.

"What, a cake the size of a Lamborghini?" Cathie asked.

"Gown, bridesmaids' gowns, reception, food—"

"That you can't eat!" Marc groaned.

"Honeymoon expenses, liquor for the open bar, caterers, waiters, waitresses—"

"A church to buy from the Catholics."

The others were used to my one-sided conversations with Cathie, but Marc was still shaking his head in that 'women are fucknuts' way that all males mastered by age three.

"None of these are working," I told the attendants. I wasn't referring to the dresses, either. "And my friend is tired. I think we'll have to try another time."

"I'm fine," Jessica rasped.

"Shut up," Marc said.

"You don't look exactly well," Laura fretted.

"Aren't you supposed to go back to the hospital soon?"

"Shut up, white girl."

"If I ever said 'shut up, black girl,' you would land on me like the wrath of the devil herself." Laura paused. "And I ought to know."

"Stay out of my shit, white girl."

"If you're ill, you should be in the hospital."

"Cancer isn't contagious, white girl."

"It's very selfish of you to give Betsy something else to worry about right now."

"Who's talking to you, white girl? Not her. Not me. Don't you have a soup kitchen to toil in? Or a planet to take over?"

Laura gasped. I groaned. Jessica was in an ugly mood, but that was no reason to bring up The Thing We Didn't Talk About: namely, that the devil's daughter was fated to take over the world.

Before the debate could rage further, the attendant cut in. "But your wedding is only a few months away. That doesn't leave us much—"

"Cram it," I snapped, noticing the gray pallor under Jessica's normally shining skin. "Laura, you're right. We're out of here."

Chapter 3

But all that stuff at the bridal shop happened months ago, and I was only thinking of my friends because I was all alone. Worse: all alone at a double funeral.

My father and his wife were dead.

I had no idea how to feel about that. I'd never liked the Ant—my stepmother—a brassy, gauche woman who lied like fish sucked water, a woman who had shoved my mother out of her marriage and shattered my conception of happily ever after at age thirteen.

And my father had never had a clue what to do with me. Caught between the daily wars waged between the Ant and me, and my mom and the Ant, and the Ant and him ("Send her *away*, dear, and do it *right now*"), he stayed out of it altogether. He loved me, but he was weak. He'd always been weak. And my coming back from the dead horrified him.

And she had never loved me, or even liked me.

But that was all right, because I had never liked her, either. My return from the dead hadn't improved our relationship one bit. In fact, the only thing that had accomplished *that* trick was the birth of my half brother, BabyJon, who was mercifully absent from the funeral.

Everybody was absent. Jessica was in the hospital undergoing chemo, and her boyfriend, Detective Nick Berry, only left her side to eat and occasionally arrest a bad guy.

In a horrifying coincidence, the funeral was taking place where my own funeral had been. Would have, except I'd come back from the dead and gotten the hell out of there. I was not at all pleased to find myself back, either.

When I'd died, more than a year ago, I'd gotten a

look at the embalming room but hadn't exactly lingered to sightsee. Thus, I—we—were sitting in a room I'd never seen. Sober dark walls, lots of plush folding chairs, my dad and the Ant's pictures blown up to poster size at the front of the room. There weren't coffins, of course. Nothing that might open. The bodies had been burned beyond recognition.

"—a pillar of the community, and Mr. and Mrs. Taylor were active in several charitable causes—"

Yeah, sure. The Ant (short for Antonia) was about as charitably minded as that little nutty guy in charge of North Korea. She threw my dad's money at various causes so she could run the fund-raising parties and pretend she was the prom queen again. One of those women who peaked in high school. It had always amazed me that my father hadn't seen that.

I looked around the room of mostly strangers (and not many of them, either, despite the two of them being "pillars of the community") and swallowed hard. Nobody was sitting on either side of me. How could they? I was here by myself.

Tina, Sinclair's major domo, had gone on a diplomatic trip to Europe, to make sure everybody over there was still planning to play nice with everybody over here. The European faction of vampires had finally come to visit a few months ago, murder and mayhem ensued, and then they got the hell out of town. Me? I thought that was fine. Out of sight, out of mind . . . that was practically the Taylor family motto. Sinclair the worrywart? Not so much.

Since Sinclair and I were wrapping up wedding arrangements, Tina had agreed to go. Since Tina was never very far from Sinclair, a solo trip for her was sort of unheard of. But her exact last words as she left the house were, "What could possibly go wrong in two weeks?"

Famous friggin' last words.

Chapter 4

I stared at the poster-sized picture of Antonia Taylor, the Ant, which was grinning at me. *Right* at me. I swear, the eyes in her picture followed me whenever I moved. It was on an easel, beside my dad's picture.

I recognized my dad's pic—it had been taken by the Minneapolis Chamber of Commerce when he and the Ant won some useless award that he bought her. The Ant's photo was from Glamour Shots. You know the kind: smokey-eyed, with long fingernails and teased hair.

"—truly found happiness in their later years—"

Barf. I didn't know whether to just roll my eyes or to laugh. Given the circumstances, I did neither.

Sinclair had disappeared a day after Tina left the country. I assumed he was still sulking about our constant bickering and had decided to avoid the thing that was Bridezilla. And in truth, I was a little glad to get a break myself. I wanted to love the bum, not fantasize about staking him. And I missed our lovemaking. Our . . . everything. I was just as sorry he was gone as I was relieved.

Not to mention, I was too proud to call his cell and tell him what had happened to my dad and his wife. That would be like asking him for help. He'd be back on his own, without me calling him, the fuckhead. Any day now. Any minute.

There weren't any windows in the room, which was a shame as it was a gorgeous summer day in Minnesota, the kind of day that makes you forget all about winter. Big, fluffy marshmallow clouds and a beautiful blue sky, more suited to picnicking than funerals.

It was kind of weird. If the occasion called for a double funeral, wouldn't it also call for thunderstorms? The day *I* died was cloudy and spitting snow.

Plus I'd gotten fired. And my birthday party had been canceled. It had all been properly disastrous.

"—truly a tragedy we mortals cannot comprehend—"

At last, the minister had gotten something right. Not only could I not comprehend it, I couldn't shake the feeling it was a sick practical joke. That the Ant was using her fake funeral as an excuse to break into my house and steal my shoes. Again. That Dad was on the links, chortling over the good one he'd put over on us. Not dead in a stupid, senseless car accident. Dad had stomped on the accelerator instead of the brake and plowed into the back of a parked garbage truck. Immovable force meets crunchable object. Finis for Dad and the Ant.

The other Antonia I knew, a pseudo-werewolf, had vanished with her mate, George—er, Garrett, the day after Sinclair had left. That didn't surprise me. Although Antonia couldn't turn into a wolf during the full moon (causing ridicule among her pack, and eventually driving her to us), she was still a werewolf bred and born, and had a werewolf's natural need to roam.

She'd been complaining of splitting headaches right before she left (rather than change, she could see the future, but it wasn't always clear, and the visions weren't always welcome). She'd been, if possible, bitchier than usual, while entirely close-mouthed about what might really be bothering her. Garrett was the only one who could stand her when she was like this.

A word about Garrett. Nostro, the old vampire king—the one Sinclair and I had killed—had liked to starve newly risen vampires. And when that happened, they turned feral. Worse than feral . . . animals—scrambling about on all fours and never showering or anything. They were like rabid, flesh-eating pit bulls. Two-hundred-pound, rabid, flesh-eating pit bulls.

Laura and Sinclair and Tina had insisted I stake the lot of them. I'd refused—they were victims and couldn't help their unholy craving for human flesh. And I'd been vindicated, I think. By drinking my blood (yurrgh!), or my sister's blood (better, but still yucky), Garrett (known back then as George) had recovered his humanity. Even better, he had become capable of love with Antonia.

So Garrett seemed fine now. But I didn't know enough about Fiends, or vampires (shit, I'd only been one for little more than a year) to try another experiment, and so a cute loyal vamp named Alice cared for the other Fiends, and Antonia and Garrett kept each other out of my hair.

Maybe someday soon, I'd ask Laura if she'd let another Fiend suck her blood, but now was definitely not the time.

All the cars driving by outside (stupid Vamp hearing!) were distracting me from the insipid service preached by a man who clearly had never met my dad or his second wife.

Once again I was struck by the fact that, no matter what rotten thing happened, no matter how earth-shaking events became, life (and undeath) went on. People still drove to and from work. Drove to the movies. Drove to doctors, airports, schools. Hopefully none of *them* were getting the accelerator mixed up with the brake.

I stifled a sneeze against the overwhelming scent of too many flowers (Chrysanthemums, ugh! Not to mention, the Ant hated 'em), embalming fluid (from one of the back rooms, not Dad and the Ant), and too much aftershave.

If nobody else was going to say it, I would: being a vampire was not all it was cracked up to be. Even though it was 7:00 p.m., I had sunglasses on for multiple reasons. One, because the lights, dim as they were, made me squint. Two, if I caught the gaze of an unmarried man, or an unhappily married man, he'd more than likely slobber all over me until I coldcocked him. Stupid vampire mojo.

Most annoying, one of my few blood relatives (I had three: my mother, my ailing grandfather, and my half sister), Laura, wasn't there either. She hadn't known my father at all, had only recently met her birth mother, the Ant (the devil had possessed the Ant long enough to get her pregnant and then decided childbirth was worse than hell), and so busied herself with interesting logistics like the wake and the burial arrangements.

Cathie the ghost had also disappeared—just for a while, she told me nervously. Not to heaven, or wherever spirits vamoosed to. Her whole life she'd never been on a plane, never left the state of Minnesota. So she had decided to see the world, and why not? It wasn't like she needed a passport. And she knew she was welcome back here anytime.

"—perhaps this is the Lord's way of telling us to get yearly driver's exams over the age of fifty—"

I smoothed my black Versace suit and peeped down at my black Prada pumps. Both very sensible, very dignified, the former was a gift from Sinclair, the latter a Christmas present from Jessica four years ago. If you get the good stuff and take care of it, it'll last forever.

Just thinking of Jessica made me want to cry—which made me feel like shit. I was sitting through a double funeral totally dry-eyed, but the thought of my cancer-riddled best friend was enough to make me sob. Thank goodness Marc, an MD for a Minneapolis emergency ward, was taking care of her.

I mean, *had* been taking care of her. Once he made sure Jessica was squared away, Marc had disappeared, too. That was more alarming than anything else, funerals included: Marc Spangler did not have a life. He didn't date. He didn't sport fuck. His life was the hospital and hanging around vampires.

I'd been calling his cell for days and kept getting voice mail or, worse, no signal at all. It was like he'd gone to Mars.

"—the comfort of many years of mutual love and affection—"

Oh, fucking blow me. Mutual credit lines and many years of the Ant seducing my dad and then begging for a fur coat. He'd married her for lust, and she'd married him for his money. And on and on and on, and never mind the cost to my mother's heart, or soul, and never mind that it had taken Mom the better part of a decade to pick up the pieces.

And thinking about the good Dr. Taylor (doctorate in history, specialty: the Civil War; subspecialty: the Battle at Antietam), my mom wasn't here, either. I knew she and my dad hadn't been on good terms for years, and I knew she cordially loathed the Ant (and believe me, the feeling was sooo mutual), but I thought she might come so I'd have a hand to hold.

Her reply to an invitation to the funeral was to quirk a white eyebrow and throw some Kehlog Albren my way: " 'Sometimes the best of friends can't attend each other's funerals.' And your father and I were not the best of friends, dear, to say the least."

In other words: *Nuts to you, sugar bear.*

But she was helping in her own way, taking care of BabyJon. I'd go see them after. Only BabyJon's sweet powder smell and toothless (well, semitoothless; he had three by now), drooly smile could cheer me up right now.

I sighed, thinking of the empty mansion waiting for me. Even my cat, Giselle, had gone on walkabout. Normally I didn't care. Or notice. But it was scary staying in the big place by myself. I wished Sinclair would come home. I wished I wasn't still so mad at him I couldn't call him. Most of all, I wished—

"The interment will be at Carlson Memorial Cemetery," the minister was saying. "For those of you who wish to follow the deceased, please put on your headlights."

—that this was over.

I stood and smoothed my black dress, checked my black pumps and matching hose. Perfect, from head to toe. I looked exactly like a smartly dressed, yet grief-stricken, daughter. I wasn't going to follow my dead father to Carlson Memorial, though, and never mind appearances. *My* headstone was there, too.

I followed the mourners out, thinking I was the last, only to stop and wheel around at a whispered, "Your Majesty?"

I recognized her at once. Any vampire would. I was even supposed to be afraid of her (every vampire was). Except I wasn't. "Do not, do *not* blow my cover," I hissed to Marjorie, who looked like a librarian (she was) but was also an eight-hundred-year-old vampire.

She was dressed in sensible brown shoes (blech), a navy blue skirt, and a ruffled cream blouse. Her brown hair was streaked with gray, and her pale face was played up with just the right amount of makeup. "Forgive my intrusion, Majesty."

"What are you doing at a funeral home, anyway? There's probably a whole back room full of Bibles in this place."

Marjorie grimaced at "Bibles," but readily answered. "I read about the accident in the paper and came to pay my respects, Majesty. I regret the deaths of your father and mother."

"She was *not* my mother," I corrected out of years of habit. "But thanks. That's why you're lurking? To pay your respects?"

"Well, I could hardly sit through the service."

I almost giggled at the image of ancient Marjorie, probably the oldest vamp on the planet, cowering in the vestibule with both hands clamped over her ears, lest she hear a stray "Jesus" or "the Lord works in mysterious ways."

I, if I may be immodest for a brief moment, could hear any religious epithet, prayer, or Christmas carol. It was a perk of being the vampire queen.

"If you need anything, you will please call on me," she insisted.

Oh, sure, Marjorie. I'd love to go to the warehouse district and hang around in the vamp library, checking out thousand-year-old dusty tomes and being more depressed than I already am. I avoided that place like most vamps avoided churches. Even in life, I'd never been a fan of libraries.

Luckily, Marjorie took care of all that tedious stuff for Sinclair and me. And even more luckily, she had zero interest in grabbing power. She'd lived through three or four kings (I think . . . I was vague on blood-sucker history) and had been content to putter among her stacks while they wreaked their reigns of terror. She had outlasted them all. I wondered idly if she would outlast me and Sinclair. Would she even remember us, two thousand years from now?

As stiff as she was, I had to admit it was nice to see her. At least somebody had bothered to show up, even if it was a vampire.

"Are you going to the cemetery?"

And see my own grave again? Not a chance in hell. But all I said out loud was, "There's nothing for me there."

Marjorie seemed to understand and bowed slightly as I turned on my (elegant) heel and left.

45

Chapter 5

I had heard the car turn in the drive, of course (sometimes I could hear a cricket from a mile away), but took my time walking to the door and listening to the increasingly frantic hammering.

Finally, after growing weary of my passive aggressiveness, I opened my front door and immediately went for the kill. "Thanks for all the support at the funeral, *Mom*. Really helpful. Why, with you there I didn't feel like an orphan or anything! Having a shoulder to lean on and all was such a comfort."

My mother brushed by me, BabyCrap™ (an

established property of BabyJon™) in tow. She smelled like burped up milk. She was wearing a blue sweater (in summertime!) and plum-colored slacks, with black flats. Her mop of curls was even more a mess than usual.

"By the way," I said cheerfully, "you look like dried up hell."

She ignored that. "A funeral service is no place for an infant," she panted, struggling to manage all the paraphernalia. It was amazing . . . the kid wasn't even a year old, and he had more possessions than I did.

Mom thrust BabyJon at me and I bounced him in my arms, then kissed the top of his head. I might have been pissed at her, but damn, I was glad to see *him*.

"You missed a helluva party," I said dryly.

"No doubt." Mom puffed white curls off her forehead. "Your father was all about parties. That's why he was foolish enough to ingest a magnum of champagne and then go joy riding into the back of a garbage truck with your stepmother."

Hey, they needed a break from all the selfless charity work. I paused, gauged what I was thinking, and then shelved it. *Nope. Too soon for jokes.* They'd only been in their graves for half an hour. Maybe by tomorrow . . .

"How are you holding up, dear?"

"Like you care!"

She scowled at me, and I almost giggled. Hadn't I seen that scowl enough times in my own mirror? But I remained a stone. "You've had a difficult day . . ."

"And you'd know this how?"

"But my day hasn't exactly been a day at the zoo, either. So answer my question, young lady, or you'll find you're not too big to spank." This was laughable, since I could break my mom's arm by breathing on it.

"Well?"

"I forgot the question," I admitted.

"How was the funeral?"

"Besides my entire support system, present company included, abandoning me in my most dire time of need?"

"I think *your* death was your most dire time of need," she corrected me. "And the only ones who abandoned you then are underground now."

This was true, but I was in no mood for logic. "And you didn't even say good-bye. I know you didn't like them, but Jesus!"

And why were we screaming at each other in the foyer? Maybe I was still too mad to make nicey-nice hostess, even to Mom, whom I usually adored. How could I not adore someone who welcomed her daughter back from the dead with open arms?

"Someone had to watch your son," she replied sharply. "And it's not as though you have no friends. Where *is* everybody, anyway?"

"The question of the day," I muttered. No way was I telling her Sinclair and I were fighting—she liked him, if possible, more than she liked me. And she'd worry herself sick about Jessica. And she didn't know Marc or Laura that well, or the others at all.

Then the full impact of her words hit me like a hammer upside the head. "Someone had to watch my *what?*"

"Jon."

"What?"

She pointed at my half brother, as if I'd forgotten I was holding him in my arms. In fact, I had. "Your son. The reading of the will? Yesterday? Remember?"

"You know full well I wasn't there. My nails were a mess, and it's not like the Ant was going to let Dad leave me a damned thing. So I gave myself a manicure in Wine Cordial."

My mother sighed, the way she used to sigh when

I told her my middle school term project was due later in the morning, and I hadn't even started yet. "In the event of their deaths, you're his legal guardian. They're dead. So guess what?"

"But—but—" BabyJon cooed and wriggled and looked far too happy with the circumstances. I couldn't decide whether to be thrilled or appalled. I settled on appalled. "But I didn't want a baby like *this*."

"Like what?"

"Like—you know. Via the vehicle of death."

Mom frowned. "What was that again?"

"I mean, I wanted my own baby. Mine and Sinclair's baby."

"Well, you've got this one," she said, completely unmoved by my panic.

"But—"

"And you certainly have the means to bring him up properly."

"But—"

"Although I wonder . . . will he get his days and nights confused, living with you two as parents?"

"*That's* the burning question on your mind? Because I can think of a few dozen other slightly more pressing ones!"

"Dear, don't scream. My hearing is fine."

"I'm not ready!"

"You're still screaming. And no one ever is, dear."
She coughed. "Take it from me."

"I can't do it!"

"We all say that in the beginning."

"But I really *really* can't!"

"We all say that, too. Well, the first twenty years,
anyway."

I thrust him toward her, like I was offering her a
platter of hors d'ouevres. "*You* take him!"

"My dear, I am almost sixty years old."

"Sixty years young," I offered wildly.

Mom shot me a black look. "My child-rearing days
are over. You, on the other hand, are eternally young,
have a support system, a rich best friend, a fine soon-
to-be-husband, legal guardianship, and a blood tie."

"And on *that* basis I'm the new mom?"

"Congratulations," she said, pushing the baby back
toward my face. His great, blue googley eyes widened
at me, as his mouth formed a drool-tinged O. "It's a
boy. And now, I have to go."

"You're *leaving*?" I nearly shrieked.

"I'm supposed to visit your grandfather in the

hospice this afternoon. You remember your grandfather, dear? Lest you accuse others of neglect."

"I can't believe you're leaving me like this! I have
three words for you, Mother—state-funded nursing
home. Do you hear me? STATE-FUNDED NURS-
ING HOME!!!" I yelled after her, just as BabyJon
yarked milk all over my beautiful black designer suit.

Chapter 6

The kitchen phone rang, and I ran toward it, stopping to plop BabyJon in his port-a-crib (a subsidiary of BabyCrap™) on the way, where he promptly flopped over on his back and went to sleep. Yeah, well, dead parents were exhausting for everybody.

I gave thanks for all the junk we'd bought when he'd been born, hoping to have occasional chances to babysit. *Babysit,* not raise him to adulthood! But because of my precautions, we had diapers, cribs, formula, bottles, baby blankets, and onesies up the wazoo.

It was funny, the Ant had only warmed up to me when she saw how much BabyJon liked me. As a newborn, he screamed almost constantly from colic (or perhaps rage at the decor of his nursery) and only shut up when I held him. Once the Ant saw that, I was the number one babysitter.

Sinclair had not been pleased. But I wasn't going to think about Sinclair, except how much I was about to *yell* at him when I got him on the phone.

The thought of surprising Sinclair with this kid, I have to admit, gave me a certain perverse pleasure. It salved the terror I felt at the sudden responsibility.

I skidded across the floor and snatched the phone in the middle of the sixth ring. "Hello? Sinclair? You bum! Where are you? Hello?"

"—can't—cell—"

"Who is this?"

"—too far—can't—hear"

I could barely make out the words through the thick static. "Who! Is! This!"

"—worry—message—country—"

"Marc? Is that you?"

"—no other way—don't—okay—"

"Tina?"

"—back—time—"

"Dad? If you're calling from beyond the grave, I'm going to be very upset," I threatened.

There wasn't even a click. Just a dead line.

I sat down at the table, deliberately forgetting about all the times the bunch of us had sat around making smoothies or inventing absurd drinks (e.g., The Queen Betsy: one ounce amaretto, two ounces orange juice, three ounces cranberry juice, seven ounces of champagne, and let me tell you, it was heaven in a martini glass).

I thought: *Everybody's gone. Everybody.*

I thought: *How could they do this to me?*

Okay, Jessica had an excuse. Battling cancer via chemo was a dandy way to get out of social obligations. And Detective Berry—well, I didn't especially want him around. He had known, once upon a time, that I had died and come back to life. I had drunk his blood, once upon a time, and it had gone badly. Sinclair had fixed it by making Nick forget. The last thing I needed was for him to be at the same funeral home he'd come to two Aprils ago for *my* funeral.

No, it was good for Nick to be at Jessica's side when he wasn't foiling killers and petty thieves.

Same with Tina. When she left to check on the European vampires, she had no idea this was going to happen. No, I couldn't blame her, either.

But Marc? He of all people didn't have a life, and he picks now to disappear? To not call, or return calls?

Mom? (Like she couldn't have gotten someone else to watch BabyJon?)

Sinclair? The guy who knew friggin' *everything* didn't show up for the double funeral?

Laura? She rebelled against her mom, the devil, by being the most churchgoing, God-fearing person you ever saw (when she wasn't killing serial killers or beating the shit out of vampires), but she couldn't be bothered to go to a family funeral?

Cathie the ghost, on a fucking world tour?

Antonia? Garrett? Okay, I hadn't known them very long, but they did live in my (Jessica's) house rent-free. I'd taken her in when her Pack wanted nothing to do with her. When the other werewolves were scared shitless of her. And Garrett? I'd saved him from staking multiple times. But they took off on me, too.

What the *fuck* excuse did any of them have? They were supposed to be my friends, my fiancé, my family, my roommates. So why was I rattling around in this big-ass mansion by myself? Except for BabyJon, snoring in the corner? Shit, nobody even sent me flowers!

It wasn't fair. And don't tell me life isn't fair, either. Like a vampire doesn't know *that*?

Chapter 7

Oh, Your Majesty!" Tina gasped, sounding tinny and distressed on the other end of the line. "I'm so dreadfully sorry! My deepest condolences. Oh, your poor parents! Your poor family! I remember when I lost mine, and it's still as fresh as it was—"

"Me time, Tina, got it?"

"Majesty, how may I serve?"

I puffed a sigh of relief. Some things, in this last crazy week, hadn't changed. Tina had always treated me like a queen, and anyone Sinclair loved, she served with everything she had. In fact, she'd had a bit of a crush on me when we first met, until I took care of our little misunderstanding ("I'm straight as a ruler, honey") and since then our relationship had been kind of complicated: sovereign/servant/friend/assistant. She was still overseas, but at least she was answering her fucking phone.

"How is the king taking it?"

"That's just it. He's not."

"I am sure he will comfort you in his own way," she soothed. "You know as well as I that a taciturn man can be difficult even during the—"

"Tina, did you forget English when you went to France? He's not taking it because he's gone. Vamoosed. Poof. Buh-bye."

"But—where?"

"Like *I* know? We haven't, um, been getting along lately, and he went off a bit ago—"

"And you've been too proud to call him."

I said nothing. Nothing!

"Majesty? Are you still on the line?"

"You know Goddamned well I am," I snapped, taking evil pleasure in her groan at the *G*-word.

"I will call him," she said, sounding cheered to have something to do. "I will request he come to your

side at once. Whatever . . . difficulties you two are having, surely deaths in the family will supersede other
considerations."

"They'd better, if he ever wants to get laid anytime
in the next five hundred years," I threatened, but felt
better. Tina was here for me (sort of) and on the case.
She wouldn't be trapped in France forever.

Sinclair would turn up. Marc would reappear
from whatever dimension he had slipped into. Antonia would get over her snit-fit and come home, drag-
ging Garrett behind her on a leash. Jessica's chemo
would triumph over the cancer, and she'd sprint
home, bossing us around as was her wont. My life
(such as it was) would be normal again.

"How is everyone else taking it?"

"Well, that's the thing." I perched on the counter,
got comfy, and explained where everyone was. Or
where I thought they were, anyway.

Afterward there was a long, awkward silence on
Tina's end, which I broke with a faux-cheerful, "Weird,
huh?"

"Rat fuck," Tina muttered, and I nearly toppled
off the counter. Tina, ancient bloodsucking thing
that she was (she'd made Sinclair, and he was, like,

seventy!), had the manners of an Elizabethan lady and almost never swore. She was perfectly proper at all times.

"Mother fuck," she continued. "Conspirational bastard shitstains."

"Uh, Tina, I think someone else just got on the line—"

"They're all gone? All of them?"

"Duh, that's what I just—"

"For how long?"

I looked at my watch, which was stupid, as it didn't show the date. "Almost a week now."

"I'm calling the king."

"Right, I got that the first time. Fine, call him, but he'd better not show up without flowers. And possibly diamonds. Or some Beverly Feldmans! Yeah, the red and gold flats would be perfect—"

"My queen, you will not leave that house. You will—"

"Huh? What are you talking about?" Long pause. "Tina?"

Nothing. Dead line. Again.

I shrugged and hung up the phone. If the French couldn't get their act together—ever—to win a war, how could they be expected to keep the phone lines open?

A mystery for another day. For now I had to figure out a feeding schedule for my new (groan) son, visit Jess (she'd want all the gory funeral details), and leave yet another message for Marc. A busy evening, and not even nine o'clock yet.

Chapter 8

"You look like hot death," I informed my best friend cheerfully.

"Go to hell," she snapped back, then coughed. Her normally gorgeous dark skin was more grayish than ebony, and her eyes were bloodshot. But she sounded a helluva lot better than she did three days ago. They'd finally quit the chemo, so she could get better.

The horrible thing about chemotherapy, of course, is that it is poison, working by killing both cancerous and normal cells. Jessica said the cancer didn't bug her hardly at all, except for making her tired. It was the cure that fucked her up severely: vomiting, constant nausea, weight loss (and if anyone on the planet didn't need to lose weight, it was scrawny Jess). How fucked up was that, I ask you? In a hundred years, doctors will be laughing their asses off at how we, the century-old savages, "cured" cancer. I mean, why not just break out the leeches?

"The moment you barf, I am so out of here." I plopped down in the chair beside her bed and got comfy, BabyJon snuggled against my shoulder.

"I haven't barfed since suppertime, and that's because it was Salisbury Steak night."

"Who could blame you?"

"How go the wedding plans?"

"They sort of screeched to a halt," I admitted. *When you all abandoned me.*

"What? Bets, you've got to pick a dress! You've got to settle on the flowers—the florist is going out of her mind! You've got to meet with the caterer for the final tasting! You've—"

"I will, I will. There's lots of time."

"There's two weeks. Isn't Eric helping you at all?"

"He's gone. Still sulking."

"Oh, Betsy!" she practically yelled, then coughed again. "Will you just call him and apologize?"

"Me?" I yelped, loud enough to stir BabyJon, who immediately settled back to sleep. "I didn't do a damned thing. He's the one who left in a huff. Stupid runaway groom."

"He'll be back," she predicted. "He can't stay away. He can't leave you, there's no such thing for him. You're in his system like a virus."

"Thanks. That's so romantic, I may cry."

"Well, don't cry. Nick was in here a while ago all teary and junk."

"Big bad Detective Nick Berry, catcher of serial killers?"

"To be fair, you and Laura and Cathie caught the killer."

"Right, but he helped. I mean, he came to the house and warned us."

"He made me promise not to die," she said, folding her arms behind her head and looking supremely satisfied. "And I made him promise. So that's all settled."

"Can I borrow that emesis basin?" I asked politely.

"Cram it, O vampire queen. Nobody barfs but me, it's the new rule."

I grinned, but couldn't help feeling the smallest twinge of jealousy. Which was completely stupid. But . . . Nick had originally been interested in yours truly. And I'd thought he'd asked Jessica out as a way to get closer to me. In fact, that had been utter wishful thinking on my part.

I was wildly happy for Jessica, but couldn't help feel a little miffed that Nick had recovered from his unholy lust for me so quickly. Which was also stupid: the whole reason Sinclair had made him forget our blood sharing was to *make* him forget. Not to mention, I had the sexiest, smartest vampire in the world on *my* hook.

When he was talking to me, that is.

"What's with the kid?"

"You won't even believe it."

Jessica covered her eyes. "Don't even tell me. You're his legal guardian."

"Got it in one."

She looked up. "Why so glum? You've wanted a baby since you came back from the dead."

"But not like *this*! I mean, gross. Garbage trucks and incinerated birth parents? Yech."

"Well, there's plenty of room in the mansion for a baby. And you're crazy about him. And he pretty much only tolerates you. So it all worked out." She paused. "I'm sorry. That came out wrong."

"S'okay. It's always nice when someone else puts their foot in their mouth. I get tired of it sometimes."

"Really?" she asked sweetly. "It's hard to tell."

"Shut up and die."

"See? You just did it!"

I didn't answer. Instead, I jiggled BabyJon to wake him up. Since I was conked out during the day, and *alone*, if he cried during the day he was shit out of luck. This was going to be a nocturnal baby, by God.

"Better start interviewing day nannies," Jessica observed.

"There's usually a hundred people hanging around the house," I complained. "We need one more? And how can we hide all our weird goings on from her? Or him?"

"How about a vampire nanny?"

I was silent. The thought hadn't occurred to me.

Then: "No good. Any vampire would need to sleep during the day."

"But Marc, me, Cathie, and Antonia are usually around during the day."

I was silent. She had enough problems without knowing that everyone had disappeared on me.

"Maybe a really old vampire? You know Sinclair can stay awake most of the day. Find some seventy-year-old bloodsucker for the job."

"Oh, sure, what a great honor. 'Hey, ancient vampire, mind changing the shitty diapers of my half brother? And don't forget to burp him before his nappy-nap. Also, don't suck his sweet, new, baby blood.' "

"Blabbb," BabyJon agreed. He turned his head and smiled sweetly at Jessica. He really was getting cute. When he was born, he looked like a pissed-off plucked chicken. Now he'd filled out with sweetly plump arms and legs, a rounded belly, and a sunny grin. His hair was a dark thatch that stood up in all directions. Jessica grinned back; she couldn't help it.

"He's definitely growing on me," she said.

"Like a foot fungus."

Jessica's door whooshed open, and the night nurse

stood there. Luckily for me, it was a man. "I'm sorry, miss, but visiting hours were over an hour ago."

I slid my sunglasses down my nose and said, "Get lost. I can stay as long as I like."

"These aren't the droids you're looking for," Jessica added, giggling.

Like a badly maintained robot, the nurse swung around and walked stiffly away.

I propped my feet up on Jessica's bed and got comfy. BabyJon squirmed and, to divert him, I plopped him on her bed. He wriggled for a moment, then flopped over and popped his thumb in his mouth, his deep blue eyes never leaving my face.

"So, dish. How was the funeral?"

"Gruesome. And filled with lies."

"So, like the Ant was in life?"

I laughed for the first time in two days. God, I loved her. That chemo was going to work. Or I would *not* be responsible for my actions.

Chapter 9

The phone rang (at 1 a.m.!), and I lunged for it. "Sinclair? Hello? You rat bastard, where the hell have you—?"

"Is this the head of Antonia's den?" a deep male voice asked.

I was flummoxed. It was a week for weird phone calls, barfing best friends, and fucked up funerals.

"Which Antonia?"

"The only Antonia. Tall, slender, dark hair, dark eyes, werewolf who can't Change?"

"Oh, the live one! Yeah, this is her, um, den."

"Explain yourself."

I was having major trouble following the conversation. "Explain what?"

"She has not checked in this month. As her pro tem Pack leader, you are responsible."

"Responsible for what?"

"Her safety."

"What's a pro tem what's-it?"

"Do not play the fool, vampire."

"Who's playing? And how'd you know I was a—I mean, who are you calling a vampire?"

"I gave Antonia leave to den with you under strict conditions. You are breaking those conditions."

"What conditions are you—?"

"Produce her at once, or suffer the consequences."

"*Produce* her? She's not a manufactured good! Who *is* this?"

"You know who this is."

"Dude: I totally completely do not."

"Your attempts to act an idiot will not sway me from my course."

"Who's acting?" I cried. "Who are you, and what the *hell* are you talking about?"

There was a long pause, punctuated by heavy

breathing. Great. A prank call from a pervert. "Very well," the deep voice growled. *Really* growled; I could feel the hairs on the back of my neck trying to stand up. "Be it on your head and suffer the consequences."

Click.

Story of my life, this week.

I stared at the now-dead phone, then threw it at the wall hard enough for it to shatter into a dozen pieces.

Chapter 10

The next evening, after feeding BabyJon his 10 p.m. bottle, burping him, and plopping him into the playpen in the kitchen, I took the new phone out of the box (thank goodness for twenty-four-hour Walgreens).

I had literally just hooked up, and hung up, the phone when it rang, making me jump right out of my skin. I snatched up the new receiver.

"What freak is calling me now?"

"Only I, Your Majesty."

"Tina! You sound tinny. Still in France?"

"Still. And worse: I have been unable to raise the king."

Raise him at poker? was my wild thought. "What?" I asked, my word of the week.

"He has never, in seventy-some years, not returned a call, or a letter, or a telegram, or a fax."

"Well. He was pretty grumpy when he left."

"Grumpy." Tina let out a most unladylike snort, almost as startling as when she was swearing like—well, me. "I dislike this. I dislike this extremely. I will be returning on the next flight."

"But what about the European vamp—"

"Hang them. Hang them all. This is much more distressing. Besides, there's not much to do here. After the show you put on a few months ago, they're quite terrified of you."

I smirked and buffed my nails on my purple tank top. It was all the sweeter because it was true: they'd seen me pray, and that had been enough for them.

"On the next flight? How are you gonna pull *that* off? Isn't it, like, a twenty-hour flight? Some of it during daylight hours?"

"I'll travel the traditional way, of course. In a coffin

in the cargo hold. Our people here will forge a death certificate and other appropriate paperwork."

I shuddered and gave thanks, once again, that I was the queen, and not a run-of-the-mill vampire. Don't get me wrong; I'd prefer to be alive. But if I had to be dead . . . "Tina, that sucks."

"Recent circumstances are highly suspect. The king would not leave you for so long—"

"It's only been a few days—"

"—nor would he ignore my messages. Something is wrong."

"He doesn't want to wear the navy blue tux I picked out?" I guessed.

"Majesty. This is serious."

I shrugged, forgetting she couldn't see me. "If you say so."

"Until I return, do not answer the door. You will not try to contact anyone who has gone missing. You will not answer the phone unless the caller ID tells you it is me." Her subservient tone was long gone; this was a general thinking fast and issuing orders. "Your Majesty, do you understand me?"

"Uh, sure. Simmer."

"I will simmer," she hissed, "when I get a few heads

on sticks. And the devil pity the rat fuck who gets in my way."

"Yeesh."

"Heads. On. Sticks."

"I got it the first time."

On that happy note, she hung up.

Chapter 11

I broke one of the rules less than twenty-four hours later. I blamed sleep deprivation. Despite my efforts over the last three days, BabyJon still had the whole "stay awake at nighttime" thing a little mixed up. (But then, so did I.)

Small wonder. The Ant, Satan rest her soul, had stuck him with night nannies all the time, and they had encouraged him to sleep so they could goof off.

I groped for the bedside phone, forgetting to check the caller ID. "Mmph . . . lo?"

"—can—hear—"

For a change, I actually identified the crackling voice. "Marc! Where the *hell* are you?"

"—can't—make—drop—"

"Are you hurt? Are you in trouble?"

"—trouble—fucked—death"

"Oh my God!" I screamed, instantly snapping all the way awake. I glanced at the bedside clock; four-thirty in the afternoon. In his port-a-crib, BabyJon snored away. "You *are* in trouble! Can you get to a computer? Can you send me an e-mail? Why aren't you answering *my* e-mails? Tell me where you are, and I'll come get you!" *With a baby in tow*, I neglected to add.

"—can't—worry—trouble—"

"Where are you?" I hollered.

"—dusk—dark—come—"

"I'll come, I'll come! Where *are* you?"

"—see—stars—"

"Marc?"

"—worried—"

"Marc?!" I was yelling into a dead line.

That was it. That was *it*. I threw back the covers of my lonely bed, trying not to realize that things were getting mighty fucking weird (and failing), and got dressed with amazing speed.

I plucked a sleepy, wet, yawning BabyJon from his crib, changed him with vampiric speed (he seemed surprised, yet amused), grabbed the diaper bag and some formula, and headed for the bedroom door to beat feet for Minneapolis General, Oncology Ward. I was breaking rule number two, and I didn't give a tin fuck. Not for the rules of ordinary man was I, the dreaded vampire queen. No indeed! I was—

My computer beeped. Rather, Sinclair's computer beeped (what did *I* need a computer in the bedroom for? We only had, like, nine offices). The thing hadn't made a peep in days, so for a long moment, all I did was stare. It beeped again, and I lunged for it, ignoring BabyJon's squawk, and saw the YOU'VE GOT MAIL icon pop up.

I clicked on it (Sinclair had set the thing up so I could use it whenever I wanted), hoping. He knew it was in our bedroom, he knew I'd hear the chime wherever I was in the house, ergo it had to be from—

My sister, Laura.

Grumbling under my breath, I read the e-mail.

Betsy,

I'm dreadfully sorry I was unable to attend the funeral of your father and my mother. I was, as you know, occupied with the arrangements for the wake and the burial, as well as helping your mother with the baby, but deeply regret my unavoidable absence. I do hope we can get together soon. Please call me if you need anything, or if you run into trouble.

God bless,

Your loving sister,

Laura

"And they that know thy name will put their trust in thee: for thou, Lord, hast not forsaken them that seek thee." (Psalms 9:10)

"Yeah, yeah, yeah," I said aloud. "Verrrry helpful." But I was all talk. At least someone hadn't forgotten me, left the country, or disappeared. Or gotten cancer.

Or if you run into trouble? What did that mean? It was almost like she knew things were getting weirder by the second. Which of course she couldn't. We hadn't even spoken until the day before the funeral, and that was all Ant stuff, not Jessica and Marc and Sinclair and Antonia and Garrett stuff.

I shoved the thought out of my head. Of all the people I had to worry about, Laura was so *not* one of them. Even if she was, according to the Book of the Dead, fated to take over the world. She was a good kid

(when she wasn't killing vampires pretty much effortlessly)

with a steady head and a kind heart

(when she wasn't killing serial killers),

and she was the definitive good girl

(even if she was the devil's own).

So there. Dammit.

I said it out loud, just to cement the idea into my head. "So there. Dammit!"

"Blurrgghh," BabyJon agreed, kicking his footie pajama feet into my hip bones.

"Ready for a trip, baby brother?"

"Yurrgghh!"

"Right. Onward, and all of that."

Chapter 12

I was so used to pouring out my troubles to Jessica—I'd been doing it since seventh grade—that I was actually shocked to find a bunch of doctors and nurses clustered around her bed. I couldn't even see her, much less talk to her. Not to mention, usually there was just one nurse, and that was only if it was time for a new bag of death.

Nick was standing off to one side, watching with his jaw clenched so tight I could see the muscles in his cheek jumping.

He saw me and said dully, "They're doing another

round of chemo. She's something of a nine-day wonder. *Everyone's* been invited."

"But—" Shocked, I shifted BabyJon to my other shoulder, for once praying he wouldn't wake up. "But she just had a round of it!"

"It's a hard cancer to kill."

"But—but—I have to tell her . . . um, stuff." *Careful*, I said to myself. Nick's poor scrambled brains didn't need any more clues that things weren't normal at the House O' Vampires. "I mean, I came to talk to her."

"Well, you can't." Clearly distracted, he ran his hands through his thick blond hair. Even though his black suit was rumpled and he had a ketchup stain on his navy blue shirt, he looked like a million bucks: swimmer's build, long legs, sharp, Norwegian features—cheekbones you could shave with!—and ice blue eyes. Before I'd died, he'd been the closest thing to a boyfriend I'd had for years. And we hadn't been that close, frankly. Friendly, not friends.

See, the Fiends had attacked me outside of Kahn's Mongolian Barbeque (this was long before I knew what a Fiend was). And like a good citizen, I reported the assault to the police. Nick had helped me look through mug shots, and we'd shared a Milky Way. That was it. The big romance. It was only after I rose from the dead (after getting creamed by a Pontiac Aztec) that I put two and two together.

Not that Nick knew any of this, and not that I had any plans to enlighten the good detective.

"They're not letting anybody talk to her," he was saying, bringing me back to the present with a yank. "But I want to talk to you."

My heart instantly went out to him. Sure, I loved Jessica as much as I loved Sinclair and Manolo Blahniks. But she and Nick had gotten pretty tight over the last few months. This couldn't be easy for him, either.

"Sure, Nicky, honey." I took his elbow and led him out into the hall. "What's on your mind?"

"In here," he said, gesturing to another room. I stepped in after him and saw it was an empty patient's room. "Put the baby on the bed."

Somewhat puzzled, I did so. BabyJon never twitched, bless him. Maybe Nick needed a hug? Maybe—oh God no—he was going to make a pass at me? Maybe he *was* only going out with Jessica because he couldn't have me! Oh my God! Like things couldn't get worse! Should I let him? Should I knock him out? Should I kill him and tell Jessica he got hit by a bus?

I turned to him and began, "Nick, listen, I don't think you're in your right—"

I stopped talking as I realized something cold and hard was pressed under my chin.

His nine millimeter Sig Sauer. (There were advantages to growing up with a mother who was an expert in small arms.)

"You're not going out with Jessica to get to me, are you?" I managed, so totally shocked that he had drawn his police-issued firearm and tucked it under my chin before I had time to realize that I couldn't move, much less slap the gun away. I was more shocked by the look in his eyes: flat rage.

"Betsy. I like you a lot. Even before you died, I liked you. But if you let Jessica die of this thing, I will shoot you in the face. I'll empty the whole clip between your pretty green eyes. I don't know much about vampires, but I bet it'll be tough for you to grow your brain back. Such as it is."

My jaw sagged in shock; the gun never wavered. "You—you *knew*?" Once Jessica got over the new chemo round, I was going to kill her! "And what's that supposed to mean, 'such as it—' "

"Of course I knew," he said impatiently. "I've known since that taxi driver gave his report—you remember. About a gorgeous blond woman who chased off a vampire and picked his car up with two fingers?"

"But—but—but—"

"Why didn't I say anything? Because you all took such great pains to keep it from me. If Jessica had wanted me to know, she would have told me. And I was content to wait. And then this—this *thing* happened to her. And that was the end of the waiting. So in case you missed it the first time: if you sit by and let this happen, I will make you regret the day you ever met me."

"Already regretting," I gurgled, since he was digging the barrel of his gun pretty tightly into my chin. "I already asked her if I could turn her."

"Then what the *fuck* are you waiting for? For her to vomit until she dies like Karen Carpenter? For her to be more miserable? For her to rupture the lining of her throat? For the chemo to kill more healthy cells?"

"Owwwww!" I complained, because boy, he was really grinding the Sig into my chin. "I'm not waiting for anything, Detective Demento. She said no. And that was that."

"So? You're stronger, faster than us. You can make us believe something . . . or forget." I should have been super pissed, but instead I was embarrassed and my heart actually flipped over in my chest. Because he sounded bitter, so bitter.

He leaned forward until our eyes were about four inches apart. Mine were wide, I knew, with amazement. His were slits of blue fire. "I thought I was going crazy, you know? Kept dreaming about you for months. Dreaming about you biting me and me . . . liking . . . it. Needing it."

"I didn't know," I said faintly. "I was newborn. Still am. I didn't know what I was doing to you. I'd have given anything to fix it, but I didn't know how. An older vampire fixed it."

"I *know* who fixed it," he informed me. "I dream about him, too. Dream about blowing his fucking mind-meddling head-peeping brains out. Dream about setting him on fire. Most nights I'm afraid to close my eyes."

"Nick, I'm sorr—"

"Know who fixed that? Your best friend. The one

currently engaged in the business of dying. Your hell-hound bastard lover fixed me, honey, and you're going to fix *her*."

I thought about taking the gun away. I could probably do it. Probably. Too bad I had the nasty feeling his finger was white on the trigger. I'd survived arrows to the chest, and a stake to the chest, and even a bullet to the chest. But a Sig Sauer clip to the brain? I had no idea. And I had no plans to find out. The week had been weird enough without getting shot, thanks very much.

And who would take care of BabyJon, if I were left with half a head? *I need to write a will,* I thought crazily. *Can I do that, now that I'm dead? Maybe Marjorie can help. But who do I trust to watch BabyJon—*

"I'm waiting," he whispered.

"Nick, you've gone seriously nuts, you know?"

"What can I say?" he replied, almost cheerfully. "I'm in love."

"Uh-huh." I thought about mojoing him, except I had my damned sunglasses on. I doubted he'd give me the second I needed to take them off. "Listen, Nick, I already told you twice, I can't—"

He cut me off, smiling. "Are we clear, Betsy?

Honey? Deadly sweetheart with a killer figure and long legs and green eyes to get lost in? *Are we clear?*"

"I hear you, detective. But it's her choice. Not mine. And not yours. So get that peashooter off of me before I make you eat it."

He grinned entirely without humor, but pulled the gun down and holstered it. His eyes were still flat. "Nice seeing you again, Betsy," he said cheerfully, and actually held the door for me as I picked up BabyJon and scuttled out. I didn't know which was scarier: the flat rage or the fake (or was it fake?) recovery.

What was going on with everybody?

Chapter 13

All the way home, I was practically gasping for breath. Which, as I didn't need to breathe, made me dizzy. So I held my breath for five minutes, trying to calm down. It worked. A little.

Nick knew? A Minneapolis detective *knew* I was a vampire, that my runaway groom was a vampire? How many other cops knew? Even if he was the only one (and one was waaay too many), what if he found out about Antonia the werewolf, assuming the walkabout wench ever came back? And Garrett? And if Jessica got worse or—oh God please no—died, what was he going to do? What the fuck was *I* going to do?

Mojoing him was out. Sinclair's clearly hadn't taken. Or had taken for a while and then worn off. But why? Sinclair was a pretty damned powerful vampire—old, and the king besides.

I took a yellow light way too fast, remembered BabyJon trapped—I mean strapped—in the car seat behind me, and slowed to a reasonable speed.

Why had Sinclair's "you are getting very sleepy" routine worn off? He could make people forget their own mothers. Was it because—it couldn't be. Naw. That was idiocy and worse, ego.

But . . . well, I couldn't shake the idea that because the long-prophesied queen of the vampires *(moi)* had gotten to Nick first, Sinclair never had a chance. That he maybe fixed it for a while, but my power was too strong, and eventually Nick remembered.

Naw. That was too conceited, even for me.

Although it was pretty much the only thing that made sense, unless Nick had been lying about Jess not telling him. And I knew in my dead heart that Jessica would set herself on fire before telling my secrets.

Sure, the Book of the Dead prophesied that I would be the strongest, coolest, most badass vampire in a thousand years, but I still had trouble actually grasping it, you know? Shit, sixteen months ago I was a secretary dreading her thirtieth birthday. But the Book had been right about everything else. So why not this?

Which meant, maybe the way to fix this was to mojo Nick myself.

Except I wasn't sure I dared. For one thing, he would be ready for that—for me.

For another, I wasn't keen on mind-raping my best friend's boyfriend.

And for another, what right did I have to wipe anybody's brain, even if it was dangerous not to? I wasn't God. I was just me, Betsy, one-time secretary and part-time vampire and soon-to-be married woman.

I screeched into my driveway, decamped with BabyJon, hustled through the front door and up the stairs to his nursery. Changed him, fed him, burped him, all the while trying to figure out what to do about Nick. And Jessica. And Sinclair. And Antonia. And—

The door chimes rang, and I leapt out of the rocking chair, gaining another gasping burp from my brother. I plopped him into the crib (it was 6:30 p.m.—time for his mid-afternoon nap) and hustled down the stairs.

Yippee! Who would it be? Did Garrett eat his key again so they couldn't get to it? Had Sinclair sent flowers? Was Nick waiting on the porch with a twelve gauge shotgun? Was it my mom? (I would consider listening to an apology.) Had Marc escaped the clutches of whatever madman had snatched him from his shift at the EW? Had Tina's coffin been rolled in from the airport? And would I have to sign for it? Was Laura stopping by with her usual sweetness to offer condolences and offer to take BabyJon off my hands?

Who cared? It was somebody, by God. I wasn't going to be rattling around the house by myself a minute longer, and that was cause for a *Hallelujah brother*!

I yanked the door open, a cry of welcome (or "Holster that sidearm, Nick") on my lips. I had just enough time to register the gleam of a wedding ring, as a fist the size of both of mine smashed into my face, knocking me back into the foyer.

Chapter 14

"Ouch, dammit!" I yelped, skidding on my back like a bug and coming to a teeth-rattling stop against the parlor door. I was splayed in a most undignified way, luckily wearing walking shorts and not a mini-skirt. And my jaw hurt like a bitch. So did my head, from where it had banged into the door. I responded to the indignity in the usual way. "Ouch. Dammit!"

While I was swearing, several people had come in (uninvited!), and all of them were looking down at me.

Wedding Ring Asshole crouched, blinked big yellow owl eyes at me, and said, "So it's true. You're a vampire. No mortal would be breathing after that one."

"Who's breathing?" I bitched. I started to sit up, but Wedding Ring Asshole quickly stood, planted his foot in the middle of my chest, and kept me flat on my back.

"Oh, now. That's just plain rude. I mean, rud*er*."

"You have much to answer for," he informed me. He was a fabulous looking fellow, I'll give the asshat that much. Tall, really tall. Brown hair and gold eyes. Not light brown, not hazel. Gold, like old coins. Not like an owl, more like . . . a lynx? A lion? Whatever. He was as powerfully built as Sinclair, and easily as tall. And I hadn't been laid in—

Never mind. Focus, Betsy! "Get your foot off my tits right now." *Nobody puts his foot on my tits.* It's a good rule to live by.

"After we talk."

"Oh, dude. You are so picking the wrong week to fuck with me."

"Produce my Pack member at once," W.R.A. demanded.

In response, I grabbed his ankle and twisted his foot all the way around. A hundred eighty degrees! Or would that be three sixty? Either way, he howled—an actual howl, like a dog!—and fell backward, losing his balance as his pulverized ankle collapsed under his weight. I flipped to my feet (well, more like staggered, but the important thing is, I was standing), momentarily triumphant.

I say momentarily because this did not make the other ones—four? five?—happy at all. I'm guessing this, because they all jumped on me at once. Unlike what happens in a karate movie, these guys didn't take turns. Nope, it was dog-pile time, with me on the bottom. (Did that make me the dog? Oh, never mind.)

I jerked my face to the side, just as a fist slammed through the floorboards where my head had been. "Wait. *Wait!*" I screamed.

Three fists (from two different people!) paused in midair, as I pulled my legs up, yanked off my saddle shoes (vintage, 1956, eBay, $296.26), and threw them into a corner.

"Okay," I said. "Go."

I blocked (barely) another fist, catching it on my crossed forearms à la Uma Thurman in *Kill Bill* (either one). I had zero martial arts training, but by God, I'd remember anything Uma did.

Fighting these guys was like dodging bullets: I could

do it, but I sure as shit had to pay attention. They were fast. They were unbelievably fast. Old vampire fast. And their smell. Their iron-rich smell. It was tough work, fighting them off and trying not to bite them at the same time.

I clawed my way back to the top of the pile through sheer force of will and, oh yeah, almost forgot, super human strength and reflexes. Not that these guys were too shabby in the area of paranormal abilities, either. Bums.

I managed to duck a few more punches and deal a few of my own, took a bite—a bite!—to the shoulder from one of them, and responded with a knee in the groin and a fist in the belly, so deep I thought I touched the guy's spine.

I took another punch to the nose (ow!) from a tank-top wearing brunette (the buzz cut was not for everyone, but it looked fabulous on her) and retaliated by stomping on the gal's ankle, smirking at the crunch, and the shriek.

I shouldn't have been smiling, I should have been pissed. Okay, I was pissed. But at least I was doing something instead of waiting for the phone to ring. If I couldn't squabble with Sinclair or bitch to Jessica, a knock-down, drag-out fight in my foyer was the next best thing.

Wedding Ring Asshole was coming for me again, and I watched in amazement as he limped, limped less, and, by the time he reached me, wasn't limping at all. I was so busy gaping I nearly forgot to duck as that ham-sized fist looped toward my head again.

Nearly. Instead I sidestepped the punch and shoved the guy so hard into the wall that the plaster (or whatever old walls are made out of) cracked all the way up to the ceiling.

Note to self: do not mention all the household repairs to Jessica until she is back on her feet.

The effect was so much fun I grabbed him by the hair and threw him into the wall again. *Wheee!*

"Don't hurt my daddy!" someone shrieked, and I was horrified to see a girl of about six standing to the side, white faced. How had I missed her? Besides the fact that the adults had all converged on me at once, like IRS agents on a small business owner?

"Are you people all crazy?" I cried. "You brought a *little girl* to a fistfight?"

I was so shocked that I didn't move fast enough to

avoid the bullets: one to my heart, two to my left lung.

"Jeannie, no!" Wedding Ring Asshole howled, as I went down and down and down and down . . .

Chapter 15

$\mathcal{I}$ opened my eyes to see a ring of faces around me. Since none of them were the faces I wanted so desperately to see, I responded in the usual way: by yelling. "Gah!"

"I think we'd better take you to the hospital," a curly haired blond woman I hadn't noticed before said. Since her hands reeked of gunpowder, and I could smell the leather of her holster (fat lot of good it did me to notice that now), I had an idea who to thank for my perforated heart. "Can you walk?"

"I think she should stay put. How would we explain

this? We're fifteen hundred miles from home. I'm not sure how many of the locals would be sympathetic."

"Well, I think—"

"*I* think you psychos better get the hell out of my house!" I then spat blood in a fine cloud that they all stared at. Nauseating, yet weirdly pretty. *Focus, Betsy.*

I tried to sit up but, weirdly, they all had their hands on my chest, even the kid. I shrugged them off (gently, for the kid's sake) and sat up. "Owwww, my heart." I furtively felt my tits. "And my lung! You bums barge in, attack the hostess, then *shoot her* in front of a child?"

"I'm no child," the child said, blinking her gold eyes at me. It reminded me of a cute little owl, and I chomped on my lip so I wouldn't smile at her. "I'm the next Pack leader." She extended a small, chubby hand. "My name's Lara."

"So pleased to meet you, darling. Nice handshake. Now get out and take your psycho guardians with you."

"I don't think you should stand," Wedding Ring Asshole worried.

"You weren't too worried about my health five minutes ago," I snapped. "And I don't think you should keep your hands on me for another half second." I climbed unsteadily to my feet. The room tilted, then steadied. Luckily I'd fed a couple of days ago—another queen perk. All vampires had to feed every day. 'Cept me. I'd snacked on a homeless guy on the way home, then picked him up (literally), ran the eleven blocks to the nearest hospital (in three minutes), and dumped him at the ER for some blankets, TLC, and hot food.

Anyway, the most-helpful drunken darling had helped me more than he knew. I heard three clinks as the bullets worked their way out of my body and fell to the wooden floor. I ignored them (must be a Tuesday!), but the other five stared at the misshapen bullets, then at me, then at the bullets.

"Out, out, *out*!" I reiterated, since they all seemed slow. Or hard of hearing. Or both.

"Truce?" W.R.A. asked, smiling warmly.

Ooooh, great grin. I ignored the twinge that brought to my nether regions and crowed, "Oh ho! Now that your tiny brains have processed the fact that I'm fairly unkillable and you couldn't beat me—or shoot me—into submission, you're all Peace Talk Central. Well, fu—" I remembered the kid. "Well, forget you."

"We just wanted to talk," one of them had the unbelievable audacity to begin, but I stomped all over that one right away.

"You all suck at talking without punching." I listened hard, but there wasn't a sound from BabyJon's room. Thank God. He'd slept through the ruckus—and the gunshots! Or he'd crawled into the laundry chute. Either way: quiet as a little baby mouse. "I mean it, ass—uh, arrogant intruders. You don't want to see my bad side."

"It gets worse than this?" one of them teased, a real cutie, with blond hair, green eyes, and a Schwarzenegger build. He was the only one who looked genuinely friendly. He was wearing faded blue jeans, beat-up sneakers, and a T-shirt that read "Martha Rules." He rubbed his chest and added, "You pack a pretty good punch, blondie. Ever think of taking up the circus life as the strong man?"

"Ever think of introducing yourselves before you mug a lady?"

"I'm Derik," the good-looking blond said, "and this is my Pack leader, Michael Wyndham." The dark-haired guy with the impressive smile and yellow eyes nodded at me. "And our alpha female, Jeannie." The curly haired shooter also nodded. "And Brendan, and Cain, and Lara—Michael and Jeannie's daughter."

All the ridiculously good-looking people nodded at me, the soul of politeness, almost like they hadn't been trying to kill me five minutes ago. And they were as amazing looking as any vampire, except they were the picture of robust, superhuman health, with blooming complexions and deep tans.

My mouth was watering just looking at them. God, they smelled so *good*. Ripe and lush, like grapes on the vine. Except for the blond gun-toter. She smelled . . . could this be right? Ordinary?

"We came looking for Antonia," Jeannie said, not taking her hand off the butt of her thirty-eight. I quickly revised "ordinary" into "gun-wielding psychobitch."

"Oh. Duh. Werewolves, right?"

"We did tell you we were coming," Michael reminded me.

"No, you dumped a totally cryptic conversation on me without even telling me your *name*, and then you hung up."

"I told you she wouldn't get it," Jeannie sighed. She snapped her holster closed, zipped her hoodie (in late June!), and I felt a little better as the gun was hidden away. Bullets couldn't kill me, but they ruined my clothes and stung like crazy.

"Antonia wouldn't have moved in with her without explaining . . . um . . . okay, it's possible my logic where Antonia's concerned is a little faulty." Michael sighed and added something puzzling while shrugging. "Rogues."

Derik smirked, Jeannie rolled her eyes, and the other three remained stone-faced, but Michael had the grace to look abashed. "I, um, like we were saying, I thought Antonia would have explained things to you. I thought you were ignoring instructions and—"

"Hello? You're her—what's it? Pack leader?"

"So she *did* tell you."

"And you never noticed that Antonia wouldn't say shit if she had a mouthful?"

"Point," Derik said cheerfully.

"I'm not the boss of her, dildo breath, just like you prob'ly weren't."

"What's a dil—" the kid began, but she shut up at a warning glance from her mother. I cringed; I'd forgotten all about her again. I reminded myself that it was their own fault for bringing a child here. *Yeah! All on them.*

I cleared my throat, which, since I had no saliva, was more of a harsh bark than anything else. Two of them jumped, and Jeannie's hand strayed toward her gun again. "Anyway. Antonia. She grew up with you bums, right? She's only been here for a few months, but she *grew up* with you bums, *right?*"

"I sense culture clash," Derik piped up. He really did look like he was enjoying himself, and it was hard not to smile back at him. He gave off friendliness like a teenage girl gave off hair spray fumes. He was like a big . . . well, puppy. "Werewolves punch first and ask questions later."

"How totally fascinating and yet not interesting to me at all."

"Unlike vampires, who never ever do anything bad," he continued, still madly cheerful.

I said nothing.

"But you stood up to our Pack and fought. So we're more inclined to listen to you now."

"Yawn," I said, since actual yawning probably wouldn't have shut them up. "So like I was saying, Antonia comes, she goes, she conquers, she bitches, she moans, she eats all the raw hamburger out of the fridge. That's what she does, that's all she does, and we sure don't get into discussions about you guys—she's made it mondo-clear that Pack business isn't any of our business." *Drives my fiancé crazy*, I thought but didn't say. "She's a ship passing in the night. She and Garrett take off *all* the time. I'm not her damned keeper. I'm her—" Uh. Friend? Ally? Thorn? Fellow bitch? Yeah, that one sounded right . . .

"Point," Derik repeated, still smiling at me. "Man, you are cute. If I wasn't married—"

"To a sorceress who'd turn her husband inside out if she saw him right now," Jeannie piped up. "I knew we should have brought her."

"She's eight months pregnant, for God's sake!"

"Still, we could have used her to fight a single vampire. This one is powerful. We could have lost someone."

I barely stopped myself from saying something stupid like, "A single vampire? Try the *Queen* of the vampires, you furry nitwits!" But it was a near thing. How was it that I was constantly either denying queen-hood or embracing it?

"Can we focus, please?" I demanded, as much of

myself as of them. "From what I'm gathering, Antonia missed checking in with you guys. So what?"

"So, we'd better sit down, don't you think? It sounds like we've got some catching up to do."

I nearly wept. "You're not going to leave, are you?"

"Not without Antonia," the kid piped up. She had a look on her face that was absolutely identical to the look on the gun-toting blonde's. If it hadn't been so weird, it would have been funny. "You didn't take her, I guess. Right?"

"Take her? Shit, I didn't even ask her to move in. She just did. Story of my life," I added in a mumble.

"Then we'd better talk," Michael said. "It seems we have a mutual problem."

"Can't we talk with you guys on the other side of the door? Or the state?"

None of them answered me. *Hell. Worth a shot.*

"Why'd you shoot me, anyway?" I asked the blonde.

"Because you were winning," she answered cheerfully.

"Swell. Last chance to leave."

They didn't move.

I thought about it, and they watched me think about it. Except for Derik and Jeannie, they all looked way too uneasy, shifting their weight and fidgeting like kids. From punching to looking freaked out in . . . what? Ten minutes? What was up with these weirdos?

"I thought you guys didn't believe in vampires," I said in a lame attempt to stall for time. At least, Antonia had said as much, way back when she'd first moved in.

"Recent events have changed our minds," the brunette—Cain—said dryly. And what kind of a name was *Cain* for a five-foot-nothing, buzz-cut brunette with a sharp fox-like face and smoothly muscled arms?

Then badass buzz-cut looked down and actually fidgeted like a little kid who needed to pee. What the hell? There were more of them than me, even if I (sort of) won the fight. Or did I? Anyway, I was outnumbered and outgunned (all my shotguns were in the gun safe in the basement). So what was their problem?

I remembered something Antonia had once said— that vampires had no scent. It took her a long time to get used to Sinclair, Tina, and me being able to sneak up on her. Obviously, my lack of scent was giving the werewolves the heebies. Ha, ha, *ha*!

I badly wanted to give the slaphappy bunch the

heave-ho, but couldn't. For one thing, I was curious to hear what they were about.

For another, I was too damned lonely to send them away.

For another, Antonia and Garrett *had* gone missing. These guys might have some light to shed.

"Kitchen's that way," I said, pointing. "Anybody want a smoothie?"

Chapter 16

I darted up the stairs, praying the werewolves wouldn't get into trouble while unsupervised, checked on BabyJon (still snoring away), then ran back down and led the werewolves and Jeannie into the kitchen just in time to grab the phone as it rang.

"S'up?"

"Betsy? It's Laura. Listen, I wanted to talk to you about—"

"Not now," I said, and hung up. I felt bad, but not too bad. She'd been one of the bums to disappear on me in a time of need, after all. And that was weirdly convenient, wasn't it? That Antonia and Garrett and Marc and Sinclair should all disappear right around the time my dad died and my half sister made herself scarce?

Naw. Crazy. But . . . weird.

Naw.

Weird.

Naw! Dammit, naw!

Great. Lonely, and now paranoid. *Oh, and surrounded by werewolves. Let's not forget that!*

"Let's see," I said, peering into the fridge. "We've got strawberries, bananas, and peaches. Also ice, for smoothies. Oh, and Antonia's left half a raw T-bone." I sniffed. "Smells fine. Prob'ly good for another day or two."

"We'll pass on the fruit."

"I could also," I added doubtfully, "defrost some hamburger for you guys."

"We're fine. Let's get down to business."

"I'm not fine. I'm thirsty as hell." I gave them all a big, toothy grin, enjoying the mutual flinch. "So it's smoothie time."

"I'd like a smoothie," Lara piped up. "Banana, please."

"Coming right up." Now it was my turn to flinch; how many times had I heard that phrase from Marc in this very kitchen as he played bartender? How many strawberry smoothies had I fixed for Sinclair? How many times had he brought me upstairs and poured said smoothie all over my—

"Banana, please!" she repeated.

I shook myself. "Sorry. Drifted off for a moment. Peel these, will you?" I said, handing Lara some bananas.

Michael cleared his throat, while his kid (cub? puppy? whelp?) stripped three bananas and tossed the skins into the sink. "So, ah. Antonia didn't check in. And she checks in at 10:00 a.m. EST on the twentieth of the month. So when she didn't, you can imagine our—"

The rest was drowned out as I hit "puree." I left it on for a nice long time, ignoring the way it felt like a thunderstorm in my head (stupid advanced vampire hearing). It was worth it just to drown out the arrogant, gorgeous asshat.

Wait. Did I say gorgeous? Sinclair, where the hell *did you go?*

Via gestures, I directed Lara to the glasses, and she brought me two. She really was the cutest thing, and I smiled at her, then dropped the grin when she didn't smile back. This was a kid older than her years, that was for damned sure. What had she said? That she was the future Pack leader? That was a lot to pile onto a—what? Seven-year-old? Eight?

A perfect miniature amalgam of her mom and her dad: his eyes, her face, their attitudes. She'd be scary as shit when she hit adolescence. Or possibly the fourth grade.

I shut off the blender, filled Lara's glass to the brim, then heard Michael droning, "—natural for us to jump to the conclusion that nefarious creatures of the night had—"

And on goes the blender again. I took my time with my own smoothie, but eventually I couldn't liquefy the fruit and ice any more and had to shut it off.

"—the fight," he finished.

Jesus! Couldn't this guy take a hint? How did Jeannie stand it? How did any of them? Luckily, *I* was not that kind of leader.

I was no kind of leader.

"Yeah, well, you were wrong, wrong, wrong." I took a large gulp of my smoothie. "Which I'm betting is a common thing with you people."

"'You people'?" the strawberry blond—the guy they called Brendan—demanded. He was about a head shorter than Michael, with the aforementioned shoulder-length strawberry blond hair, the usual-to-werewolves sculpted muscles (at least, the werewolves I'd seen), lean build, chiseled good looks, big gorgeous eyes (a kind of gold/brown in his case). They almost seemed to glow from within. *Luminous.* That was the word. "What's that supposed to mean?"

Were there no fugly werewolves? Fat ones? Near-sighted, squinty-eyed ones?

"I *said*, what's that supposed to mean?"

Mild-mannered ones?

"You carnivorous ravenous creatures of the full moon," I said sweetly. "Carrying off babies, biting people and turning them into fellow ravenous creatures of the full moon, attacking large-breasted women wearing tight T-shirts." I hailed him with the smoothie. "You know. '*You* people.'"

"Ugh!" Derik said, looking genuinely revolted. Looking, in fact, a lot like Antonia when she had told me what he was about to say. "Omnivores taste awful. Trust me. We don't eat you."

"And it's not the measles," Cain (again: What kind

of name was that for a woman?) barked. Literally. "You can't catch it. We're two different species, you high-lighted dimwit."

"Like them?" I asked, pleased, while I patted my bangs back into place. "And if we're two different species, you want to explain her?"

Lara coughed out some banana smoothie as I pointed at her.

"Uh," was all Derik got out.

"I mean, there are no zebra-tigers, right? No gorilla-giraffes? Porcupine-platypi?"

"It's . . . complicated," Michael grumped.

"Nothing you could possibly understand," Cain snarled.

"Cain."

Cain sat down and shut her mouth. *Hah!* I looked at Michael with a smidge more respect. Guy hadn't even raised his voice, and Cain was looking like a whipped hound. Really, he was a lot like Sinclair in many ways, and it was a damned shame he was m—

Stop that, Betsy.

"—mean to offend you in your own home."

"No, you certainly wouldn't want to offend me. That's coming through loud and clear, Fist Boy."

"Pack Leader Fist Boy," Brendan corrected, fixing me with a glare he probably thought was menacing. He'd never dealt with a hysterical Marc when he couldn't find a clean scrub shirt. Or Laura when she was late for church. Or Garrett when he ran out of yarn before he finished a sweater.

Or Sinclair, for that matter, at any time. My guy had only to look this pup dead in the eye, and the kid (couldn't have been a werewolf hair over twenty-two) would be his slave as long as Sinclair wanted.

As a matter of fact, *I* could probably make this kid my slave.

I actually thought about it while one of them babbled about something or other. But in the end I decided to play it carefully. They already knew I was quick and strong. That was two things too many for strangers to know about me. There was plenty of time to turn on the charm, if I needed to.

"—where they might be?"

"Who?"

"Antonia and Garrett, you twit!"

"Brendan."

Puppy Boy sat down and shut his piehole.

"So?" Michael prompted.

"What?"

Michael ran both hands through his brown hair, mussing it to no end. "So. Where. Do. You. Think. Antonia. And. Her. Friend. Are?"

"I. Have. No. Idea. That's. The. Whole. Problem."

Lara giggled. Or gurgled; she had another mouthful of smoothie. I drained the rest of mine in two gulps and got up to head for the counter.

"Not the blender again, vampire, we're begging you." Cain said it with touching, horrified sincerity; Brendan managed to look equal parts sneery and weary.

That's vampire queen, I thought. But I took pity on them. Their hearing was probably as good as mine.

Maybe better. I narrowed my eyes at them while I rinsed my glass without looking, then accidentally broke it on the faucet head. I assessed their strength, their tone, their differences from Antonia.

Antonia, who was strong but not a shape-shifter.

Antonia, who could see the future but at a horrible cost to herself, and the one she loved.

I couldn't imagine what was worse: being considered a freak by, well, other freaks, or having horrible visions that were never, ever wrong.

Is that why she was gone? Had she seen something awful

(Please God, nothing bad about Sinclair or Marc or Jessica okay, God? I'll owe you a big one, God, in Jesus's name, amen.)

and vamoosed, taking her own personal Fiend with her?

No way. Antonia was a lot of things, but she'd never run for cover. And if she did run for cover, which she'd never do, she wouldn't do it without warning me first. After all, I was her—what was it? Pack leader pro tem?

"You know," I said, sitting across from Michael, "Antonia was pretty tight-lipped about you guys."

Silence.

"She didn't talk a lot about Pack stuff." In fact, I was trying to remember a single damned thing I knew about the Pack. And I was coming up pretty close to blank. And not just because I usually tuned Antonia out five or ten seconds into her rant du jour. Well, yeah, that was probably the main reason, but, bottom line . . . "She just didn't."

"She didn't talk to me about vampire stuff," Michael volunteered. "Every month it was the same thing. Everything okay? Yes. Need anything? No. Any messages you want me to pass along? No. Anything you want to tell me about? *Hell*, no."

We all sat in silence for a few seconds. I don't know about them, but I was thinking that I was damned fortunate Antonia was able to juggle her loyalties so well. From the look on Wyndham's face, he was thinking the same thing, or close to it.

I crossed my legs and stared at my black socks. *Must remember to get my saddle shoes out of the foyer.* "She must have explained when she moved in. Didn't she?" I looked up and beheld identical puzzled expressions. "I mean, she said she had to get permission from you, and I thought it was extremely weird that a grown woman had to 'get permission' to live with us, but when I said that, all she said was that my face was extremely weird and to shut the hell up."

Wyndham and his peeps nodded. Michael added, "She had little to say about you even when she moved to the Midwest. 'I found my destiny,' she says, 'and it's with the king and the queen of the vampires. Yes, they're real,' she says."

"Don't feel bad about not believing," I told him. "I didn't believe in werewolves until Antonia showed up. And, uh, didn't change into a wolf."

"'I'm not coming back,' she says—this was her way of asking permission. 'So sell my house and cut me a check. And don't give me any shit, or I'll foresee your death and forget to mention it.'"

I had to admit, it had the ring of authenticity.

"She agreed to check in every month," Michael said, "and that was the end of it. Until, of course, we didn't hear from her. Now. Tell me, Betsy. What is a Fiend? And where can we find the one that killed our Pack member?"

Chapter 17

"Whoa, whoa, *whoa*!" I said, wishing I wasn't doing this all by myself. "Let's not jump to any conclusions, my eager little pups. Garrett would eat his own balls before he'd ever hurt Antonia, and he'd never, *never* kill her."

Derik shuddered and covered his eyes. "Must you use phrases that I'll never get out of my head? 'Eat his own balls'? Who *says* that?"

"Not to mention, it's hard to believe," Cain added.

"Believe? Why is that so hard? Now all of a sudden you're big vampire and Fiend experts?"

"Vampires aren't accident-prone?" Jeannie asked, and to her credit, it sounded like an honest question.

"Well, I am," I admitted. "But not Garrett."

"You can explain about Fiends?"

"Sure."

"There are no taboos against discussing such things with outsiders?"

"I dunno." Wyndham couldn't hide his surprise, so I borrowed a phrase from his pal Derik. "I think it's that culture clash thing again. If it'll keep you from pulling Garrett's legs off, I'll answer any question you like."

"That's a *good* thing, chief," Derik said. "Stop looking like you're expecting the other shoe to drop—on your head."

"For a ruthless despot of the undead, you're awfully charming," Michael said, and no one in the room was surprised when Jeannie's fist slipped. But he got his breath back in no time at all.

Lara asked—and received—permission to use the bathroom. Jeannie got up to accompany her. And I used the kid's absence to explain about Fiends, about Nostro and his sick-ass psycho games, about Garrett's slow recovery, about all the progress he made and how much he and Antonia loved—

"So by your own admission, this creature was sub-human only six months ago?"

"I don't know if sub—"

"Subsisting on buckets of blood, running around on all fours, and howling at the moon?"

"Physician, howl thyself," I pointed out.

"And he couldn't even talk?" Michael persisted.

"I don't know about *couldn't*. *Didn't* talk would be more accurate. But see, after he drank my blood and the dev—and my sister's, he got better. And you guys—you just don't know. I mean, the way he feels about Antonia. She's his everything. He'd ki—uh, he'd die for her."

"And she for him, I s'pose?"

"Well, it's hard to imagine Antonia getting all mushy and stuff, but yeah, I imagine she'd—" Too late, I saw the trap Michael had set for me. I shot to my feet and started to pace. "You guys, Garrett did not kill Antonia and then take off for parts unknown. There's no way. *No* way."

"Mmmm," Wyndham said.

"Hmmm," Derik added, also apparently unconvinced.

"You don't see me with my knickers in a knot,

asking you if your Pack member killed *my* guy and then took off. Did I show up, fists flying, jumping to conclusions? No." I smirked to see the Wyndhams looking uncomfortable. Except for Brendon, who glared at me.

"We've been over this," Michael said, mildly enough.

"Yeah, but now that your kid's gone, you can apologize for being totally out-of-control, foaming, slavering assholes who hit first and asked questions later."

He drummed his fingers on the table for a few seconds, and then, after a long, difficult moment (difficult for him, not for me) he said, "I apologize."

"Okay. It's totally conceivable that Antonia saw the future and got the hell out of here and that Garrett tried to stop her and so she—she—I dunno, gave him a bath in holy water and then left town on the first Amtrak headed east. That could totally happen, but I'm not getting all suspicious and paranoid, right? So there's no reason for you guys to stay beady-eyed."

"Are there any other unusual goings-on?" Michael asked, leaning forward. "Anything mysterious? Something that might lead us to answers?"

"Everything's fine," I lied. I cocked my head;

I could hear BabyJon asking for a bottle. Loudly. "And you'll have to excuse me a minute; my brother needs me."

I moved past them, and Wyndham's hand shot out and closed over my forearm. I saw the whole thing and had plenty of time to avoid him. But I didn't. His hand was really warm. I could actually feel his heart-beat through his fingers.

And he smelled—have I mentioned how frigging *delicious* these guys smelled? No wonder Garrett found Antonia irresistible. It sure wasn't her personality.

Michael's hand squeezed my arm. He was so cute, thinking he was actually holding me in place. "Betsy, really. *Is* there anything going on?"

I smiled. "Michael, you worry too much, anybody tell you? I said everything's fine, now didn't I? So don't sweat it."

On my way to the nursery, from one room and a hallway away, I heard Michael's very distinct order to Derik.

Chapter 18

Derik bounded beside me on the stairs like a big blond puppy. "It's nothing personal," he said cheerfully, keeping pace with me as I climbed the eighty zillion stairs to the nursery. "But we can't tell if you're lying or not—that whole 'no scent' thing—and it's driving the chief out of his head."

"I'll bet." I was a smidge—just a smidge—sympathetic. To go your whole life being able to tell if everyone around you was lying or not, that had to come in handy. One of the few things Antonia had mentioned was that her Pack hardly ever bothered with lying . . . there was absolutely no point.

And then to run into me, someone who could say she was a short, genius brunette and still smell fine (or not smell, as the case was), that had to be frustrating.

"So I, the most charming and handsome werewolf in all the land—"

"Should I throw up here on the stairs? Or try to wait until I can find a garbage can?"

"—will catch you off-guard with my witticism and charisma."

"And don't forget your sexy Martha Stewart T-shirt."

"Hey, hey. Don't diss my girl Martha. She could kick your fine undead ass with one homemade seashell napkin holder behind her back."

"Derik, you're seriously bent, you know that?"

He ignored me. "And then I, fearless Pack member, shall swoop down on the truth like a crow on a grub."

"Did you just call me a worm?"

"I did not," he said, following me into the nursery. "I called you a grub. Big difference. Huge!"

I laughed; I couldn't help it. The big doof probably *was* the most charming werewolf in all the land. "Dude, you really are the—eh?"

I had reached the crib, bent over, plucked BabyJon out. And was surprised to be alone. I turned and Derik was—there was no other word for it—he was cowering beside the nursery door.

"What's going on?" I asked, completely startled to see the six-foot-plus blond huddling in terror.

"I was gonna ask you the same thing. Jesus!" He forced himself to straighten, shook himself all over, then cupped his elbows in his palms. It almost looked like—it looked like the big strong badass werewolf was hugging himself for comfort. But *that* couldn't be right. "Every hair on my body is trying to jump ship right now. Least that's what it feels like. I've got the *worst* fucking case of the creeps. I—what's that?"

"This is my baby brother." BabyJon wasn't crying or anything. I had slung him over one of my hips, and he was just looking at Derik, patiently waiting for his bottle. What a sweetie. Orphaned, and hungry. And not crying! "Isn't he the cutest?"

"Keep him away from me," Derik ordered, actually backing out of the room. Guess he wasn't fond of babies. "It feels like thirteen o'clock in here."

"Derik, what the hell's gotten into you?" I followed him out into the hall, genuinely puzzled. If Michael had sent his Good Guy WereCop after me to try to fish for more info, this was a weird way to go about it. "You're acting all—"

"Don't do that!" Both Derik's hands shot out, palm up. He was—warding me off? No way. I had it wrong. I was misreading werewolf body language, or whatever. "I might have to bite you. And not in a nice way, get it? So just—aaaaiiieeeeee!"

He said aaaaiiieeeeee because at that moment he fell down the stairs. All the way down. And with my hands full of BabyJon, I had no chance to catch him. So I just stared, cringing at some of the thuds and wincing at some of Derik's more colorful language as he plummeted to the bottom.

I sighed. Then I put BabyJon back in his crib, ignoring his surprised squawk, shut the nursery door, and started down the stairs.

There was no way they were going to believe Derik fell down the stairs—all the stairs—without assistance. I assumed there was going to be another fight. Best to get it over with.

Too bad, really. Just when I thought we'd established a little trust.

Chapter 19

"Well, thanks for stopping by," I said again, and it was even more lame than the first time I said it.

Derik, upon his quick recovery, had done some fast talking to save me from another werewolf beat-down, and now they were all leaving. And not being very subtle about wanting to get the hell out of my house, either. If I hadn't felt so anxious, I would have been amused.

Derik limped past me, which was a big improvement, because he'd broken both legs when he'd hit bottom. These guys regenerated as fast as Sinclair and me . . . maybe faster. Must be their iron-rich, high-in-protein diet. Mmm . . . their yummy, yummy diet. I was drooling just watching them file past. How had I never noticed how delicious Antonia was?

Easy. When Antonia was around, Sinclair had also been around, and his blood was just fine. More than fine. We'd actually incorporated blood-sharing into our lovemaking and now, like a Pavlovian dog (or George on the *Seinfeld* episode when he equated salted cured meats with sex), all I had to do was get a whiff of someone's delicious blood and also find myself horny as hell. Which wasn't exactly—

"Why are you looking at me like that?" Derik asked, massaging his knee.

"Uh. No reason. Thanks again for visiting. And good luck picking up Antonia's scent." I'd offered to show them her and Garrett's room, let them get a whiff of the sheets or whatever, and they'd all looked at me as if I'd lost my mind.

I guess I was picturing a scene right out of a cop movie: baying bloodhounds sniffing sheets or a dirty sweater and then howling off into the night, hot on the trail. Apparently real life was different. And werewolves weren't bloodhounds.

Which was a shame, because bloodhounds were really cute.

"Crazy fucking vampire," Jeannie muttered, so softly she probably assumed I hadn't heard her.

"Don't forget your parting gifts!" I cried, sending Lara after them with a helpful shove.

"Thanks for your hospitality," Michael said without the teensiest bit of irony. We shook hands as the others filed past. He squeezed. I squeezed. He squeezed harder. So did I. I figured anybody else's hands would have been crushed to bloody powder by now. "We'll be doing some checking around town and will keep you posted," he added, slightly out of breath from our *mano a bimbo*.

"And I'll call you"—I held up the card with his cell phone number on it—"if I hear anything from either of them."

"Thanks. Have a good night."

"You, too. Bye, Derik. Cain. Brendon. Lara. Jeannie. Michael."

"Betsy," Jeannie said, "I want to make clear that I only shot you because—"

I shut the door. And since it was a big heavy door

about two hundred years old, it cut her off with a solid BOOM!

Did I think they had anything to do with everything that was going on? No. I really didn't. Werewolves weren't exactly famous for lying or subversiveness. I seriously doubted they'd—what? Snatched Antonia back, staked Garrett, then shown up at my house and staged a pretend fight, all the while playing like they had no idea where Antonia and Garrett were?

Vampires would pull that sneaky shit in a cold minute. The Wyndham bunch? Naw.

Probably naw. Their appearance today was still an awful coincidence.

It was either a really really good thing that the werewolves were in town right now, or a really really bad thing. Too bad I had no idea which it was.

I took the stairs two at a time, plucked a fuming BabyJon out of his crib, fixed a fresh bottle (he liked 'em cold, and we kept a supply in the small fridge in his room), and let the poor starving tyke have at it. While I was walking with him back to the kitchen, I wondered about Derik's extreme reaction to my half brother. Hadn't he said that his wife was pregnant? Maybe babies freaked him out.

I cuddled BabyJon closer into my side and kissed the top of his fuzzy dark head. "Guess he'd better get over that in a hurry," I told him. "Unless he likes sleeping on the sorceress's couch."

The phone rang as I got near the swinging door, and I grimaced. What fresh hell was this?

Chapter 20

"Majesty?"

"Tina? Hey, finally! Great to hear from you!" From anybody without fur, frankly. "What's going on?"

"Nothing good, Majesty, I assure you." She made a sound that from anyone but Tina would have come off sounding like a snort. "Are you well?"

"Oh, sure. A bunch of werewolves stopped by to pick a fight, but—"

"You mean they broke in?" Tina interrupted. Since she never interrupted, I assumed she had to be fairly shocked. Then I remembered her strict instructions, most (or all? I couldn't remember all of them, to be honest) of which I'd broken since we last spoke.

Lucky for me she was half a continent, plus an ocean, away. She could only scold; she couldn't strangle.

"Well, no. They didn't break, exactly. They, um, knocked."

"And you *let* them *in*?"

"Like I said. Knocked. Then, the fight. Which I won, so don't worry." I decided not to mention Jeannie "Quick Draw" Wyndham. Tina hated it when I got shot. "Turns out they thought we were being sneaky, because Antonia hasn't checked in with them."

"Um."

"But I convinced them that we hadn't done away with her or anything, using my Kissinger-like powers of diplomacy."

"Um-hum."

"Now we're buddies!" I tried to put as much enthusiasm as I could into that lie. I mean line. "Isn't that great? Even as we speak, they're scouring the town, looking for the hair of Antonia's chinny-chinchin. Wait, that was the pigs, right? That line made no sense, then. Let me think of—"

"Majesty! I must beg you to—"

"I know, I know. I've been answering the phone *and* the door. It's all gone horribly, horribly wrong, and all because I didn't listen to you." I slung BabyJon over my shoulder to burp him, tossing the now-empty bottle in the general direction of the sink. "If only I had listened." BabyJon yawned, and I knew how he felt. The lecture loometh.

"Majesty, I do not wish to alarm you—"

"Then don't."

"But I fear the king may be dead."

"See, that? I find that alarming." I whacked BabyJon a little too hard, because he groaned—then belched. I plunked him into the port-a-crib so I could pace.

"I'm sorry, Majesty, but it is the only conclusion that fits the data."

"What the hell makes you think that?"

"He would have answered me by now, Majesty. In seventy-some years, he has never *not* answered me. We have a code we use for emergencies, and the other one, no matter what is happening in his or her life, the other one must answer. And he has not."

"He blew off your super secret vampire code?"

"I realize that infantile jokes are your way of dealing with serious issues, but with all due respect, Majesty, now is not the time."

"Noted," I said, chastened.

"He is not sulking, as you think. He is not hiding. He is not shirking his duties as your groom. And more—"

"What? There's more? What?"

"He would never abandon the queen," she said quietly. "No matter how silly he thought the wedding rituals. Someone has him. Or someone has killed him."

"What—what are we going to do?"

I heard a thud and realized that Tina, from eighty zillion miles away, had punched a wall. "I. Will do. Nothing!" Another thud. She was pounding the wall like Rocky Balboa worked a punching bag. "I cannot get back to you. There are riots in France, and all flights are canceled until further notice."

"Riots?"

"Surely you saw on CNN—never mind."

"Oh, the riots! Right, right. The riots. Those pesky French riots."

She ignored my lame-ass attempt to pretend I was

up on current events. "I cannot even charter a private plane. To go by boat would take too long. I am trapped here, Majesty. And you are alone."

"Tina, it's—" *Okay*, I had been about to say, and who was I kidding? Tina, one of the smartest people I'd ever met, thought Sinclair was dead. *Ergo*, he . . . wasn't.

I would take refuge in my stubbornness. She was wrong, wrong, wrong and also needed a deep conditioning treatment. I wouldn't let the panic take hold. I wouldn't. It couldn't have me. The panic would have to find someone else to bug; *I* wasn't going to play ball. Sinclair wasn't dead. Or even in danger.

Tina was wrong. This one time, in a matter that was as important to her as it was to me, this one time she had screwed up. Who knew why? The stress of being away from home? The hassle of going through Customs via coffin? The important thing was, she was stressed out and jumping to conclusions. Because the alternative was totally beyond my grasp. I couldn't imagine a world without Sinclair in it. And wasn't that silly? Two years ago, I hadn't even known the guy existed.

"Tina, stop hitting that wall. You're going to hurt yourself."

"I did," she said dully. "I broke most of the fingers in my left hand."

"Jeez, what are you punching, cement?"

"Yes."

"Well, stop. Focus on getting back."

"But the rioters—the roads are closed, or barricaded. No one can get in or out. I cannot help you, my queen, I am stuck in this place." "Place" came out like "placc-cccce" because Tina hissed it as opposed to saying it like a person who wasn't half crazy with guilt and grief.

More riots in France! Perfect timing. So typical of France not to consider *my* needs before passing martial law.

"I know it seems tough, but they'll eventually let planes out, they've got to. For one thing, FedEx can't get there. People need their overnight packages, Tina! They want their Sephora and their cheese. The French people won't stand for it, trust me, the airports won't be closed for long. Or at least get out of the country and take a plane from a country that *isn't* rioting in the streets."

"That is . . . excellent advice, Majesty." I could hear the surprise in her voice, but couldn't blame her. It was weird enough Tina hadn't thought of it. Weirder that I had. It showed how upset she really was. And how convinced she was that Sinclair was dead, how rattled her conclusions had made her. "I will start at once. With your permission, I will not waste your time with phone calls unless I have news to report."

"That's fine, Tina."

"And, Majesty?"

"Yeah?"

"Consider now following my advice. Do not answer the phone, do not answer the door. I doubt whoever ki—"

"Don't say it!"

"—I doubt whoever detained His Majesty will be content only with him."

"That's better. *Detained.* Yep, that's the word of the day, all right. Listen, be careful."

"You took the words," she said, "right out of my mouth." And without so much as a "See ya later, gator," she hung up.

Chapter 21

*H*e is not dead.

He is not dead.

He is not dead, because if he was? I'd kill him.

But I had to face facts. Sinclair wasn't sulking. For one thing, it wasn't his style. He liked to engage, not withdraw. For another, as silly as he thought the wedding stuff was? He'd never stick me with all of the prep less than two weeks before the big day.

Well, he might stick me with it, but he wouldn't out-and-out disappear on me. Even when I thought I hated him, he'd been impossible to get rid of. Now, when we loved each other, he'd made himself scarce? Not likely.

Tina was half right: someone had snatched him. But who? And how come? And where the heck was he?

I glanced over and saw BabyJon had tired of playing with his soft blocks and toppled over on his side, one thumb corking his mouth shut. He watched me with sleepy blue eyes as I paced, as I grumbled and thought and chewed my nails and prowled back and forth.

Finally I sat down at the kitchen table, folded my hands, looked at my folded hands, and thought: *this is not a coincidence.*

I thought: *Sinclair* and *Marc* and *Antonia* and *Garrett* and *Cathie* and *Tina* and *Jessica* and *Nick* and *a double funeral* and *Laura* and *my mom? All those people either missing or deliberately absenting themselves from my life? And now, of all times? The week my dad and the Ant died? Two weeks before I married the King of the Vampires? Granted, I remember wishing everyone would leave me alone for a few days, but this was ridiculous.*

I thought: *Who killed my father and my stepmother? Because this was all just a little too neat, you know? Too neat by a damn shot.*

Didn't they know they were fucking with the

queen of the vampires? (Whoever "they" were?) Didn't they know what I—we—could do to them?

Sure they did. They just didn't care. They didn't think I was a threat; no vampire had ever thought I was a threat. They only believed me as I was killing them. And even then, the rumor spread that Sinclair had really done it. Even the European faction had taken a damn year to pay their respects.

And who was I kidding, calling myself a vampire queen? If I didn't believe the Book of the Dead said Sinclair and I were married, how could I believe it about anything else? *Can't have it both ways, Bets*, as Jessica might have said.

So who had seen my weakness, and acted?

And what the blue hell was I going to do about it?

This was, of course, assuming it was all about me.

I almost laughed. Of course this was all about me! Just not in a good way.

I picked up the phone, dialed my mom's number, and waited for her to answer. "Mom? Listen, I need a favor. The shit's hitting the fan over here, and I don't think it's safe for BabyJon. Can you take him for a couple of days?

"Mom?

"Hello?"

Chapter 22

Just what do you think you're doing, young lady?"

I stared at my mom, whose white curls were straggly in her wrath. She'd roared right over to the mansion in her Honda to kick my ass. I was just having trouble figuring out . . .

"You want to know why I'm so angry?"

"Not really."

"I'll tell you why. You are responsible for this infant." She pointed a nonmanicured index finger at BabyJon, who yawned. "You. Not me. Not your sister."

"Did Laura talk to—"

"You. And at the first sign of trouble—"

"The first?" I yelped.

"—you come running to me to kiss your boo-boos and make everything all better. Well, I can't, Betsy. You're a grown woman, and it's about time you started acting like one."

I looked at my mother, Dr. "Suburbs" Taylor, with real irritation. I hadn't felt this close to smacking her since I was fourteen and she'd caught me with her credit cards at the Burnsville Mall (she *knew* what that shoe sale meant to me!).

I was a grown woman, and it was about time I started acting like one, eh? Well, let's see. Let's think about all the things this grown woman did that Dr. Taylor, safe in her book stacks, had no clue ever happened.

There was the overthrowing of not one, but two vampire psychopaths. There was the tracking down and dispatching of the serial killer (though technically Laura got the kill claim on that one). There was taking on the responsibility of governing the vampire nation, whatever the hell that was. The tension of the European faction finally visiting, and solving *that* subsequent murder. And the zombie in my attic who showed up from God knows where, God knows why, which I had to kill. By myself.

Oh! And let's not forget about the pack of werewolves who showed up trying to tear my head off!

All right, to be fair, it wasn't her fault she didn't know about any of the above. I had made a conscious choice to leave her out of the vampire side of things, a choice wholeheartedly endorsed by Sinclair and Tina.

But the stuff she knew about was bad enough: the tension of the wedding, not to mention the funerals. Oh! And suddenly being the guardian of a baby. Almost forgot that one! And if she was vague on the details of my vampiric lifestyle, she at least knew the basics: I had died, I had come back, and my life was infinitely more complicated as a result. Oh, and my *father* had just *died*.

Ah, but the broad had a few more left. "Really, Betsy. At the first sign of trouble, your impulse is to dump your problems on someone else. You've got to grow up."

"Are you taking him for the next two days, or aren't you?"

My chilly tone must have startled her, because she

actually paused for a few seconds, then said, a tad on the meek side, "Of course I'll take him. Laura promised to give me a hand. I just wanted you to know— to realize what you—I just don't want you to get in the habit of—"

Yawn. I had no time for this. I handed her BabyJon, snug in his carrier (the base was on the front porch, where Mom would pluck it and then strap it onto her backseat), and the diaper bag with the Baby-Crap™. "Thank you. Good-bye."

Mom hesitated, glanced down at the baby, then hurriedly looked back up at me. But not so fast I didn't see the flash of distaste cross her features.

Ah-ha. And duh. Should have guessed that one. "I appreciate that babysitting the living embodiment of your late ex-husband's faithlessness can't be easy, but I'm not exactly having a fun week, either, Mother."

"I—I know, Betsy, it's just that—"

"I have work to do, Mother."

"What kind of work?"

"Just a pedicure. You know. The usual thing since I died and came back as a vampire. Thanks for helping me out of yet another frivolous jam."

"Betsy—if I spoke without thinking—"

I picked up the phone and stared at her. She clutched the car seat to her, then grimaced and eased up on her grip. BabyJon just watched her. So did I.

"Betsy, is there something you want to talk about?"

"Not anymore." I started to dial Minneapolis General. "If you'll excuse me, I need to call the oncology ward. You know, my best friend's new digs? Boy, talk about frivolous! You should hear her bitching about all the puking the chemo makes her do. Maybe I should send you over for a pep talk."

"I went and put my foot in it, then," Mom said, sounding so much more like her old, supportive self that I almost weakened. "And not only was I unfair, but I've got lousy timing, is that it? Well, you're right and I'm sorry. Other than—this—" She frowned down at the baby. "Is there another way I can help?"

"Don't be silly, Mom. I know how hard you're working this month, what with your department *not* teaching courses all summer."

"Fair enough." She started for the foyer. "When you're ready to listen to me grovel, I'll be glad to do so. For now, dear, please call me if you need anything else. And yes, I'm aware of the irony of encouraging you to call me after this argument."

"Good thing I don't have to point it out, then!" I yelled after her.

While I waited to be connected to Jessica's room, I pondered the odd series of events that led to my mother babysitting her dead rival's youngest child. I hadn't wanted to call Mom—I wasn't entirely insensitive. On that topic, anyway. And I hadn't been able to reach Laura . . . most likely because she was busy calling my mom. It sounded like they'd already had at least one conversation today, topic: BabyJon.

But it just wasn't safe around here for BabyJon right now. Shit, it wasn't safe for *me*. I'd take a lot of chances with my own safety, no problem.

But not BabyJon's, possibly the only baby, ever, who was going to be really mine.

Chapter 23

Some jerk of a male nurse wouldn't connect me (why oh why didn't my vampire mojo work over phone lines?), so I disobeyed Tina (hey, it was that kind of week), hopped in one of Sinclair's Volkswagens (my Ford was in the shop—it needed a new starter), and was at Minneapolis General in fifteen minutes. (One of the blessings of being undead? I never faced rush hour anymore.)

Sure, at 10:00 p.m. it was way past visiting hours, like I gave a rat fuck. Even when I was alive, I wouldn't have cared. Because I, Betsy Taylor, was . . . an ex-model!

The key to not getting kicked out of a given restricted area is to stride briskly and look like you have every right to be there. (I learned this my first week as a model . . . in fact, I got backstage passes to Aerosmith that way.) Being tall helped, too. And pretty.

Look, I've never made a secret of the fact that I was genetically blessed. To ignore said blessings would be like a great painter throwing away her brushes. Or Jessica not using any of her money just because she inherited it from her scumbag father. Why make life harder by not using what you had?

Anyway, I was striding down the hall toward Jessica's room, having made it past reception to the elevator bank, past several nurse's stations, and I was about thirty feet away from being home—

"Excuse me? Visiting hours are over."

I turned and smiled. Visiting Hour Enforcer smiled back. *My* smile broadened when I noticed the lack of wedding ring on Nurse Guy's finger. He was a cutie, too—about five ten, curly black hair cut short, flawless dark skin the color of expensive coffee. Big, gorgeous dark eyes, the whites almost bluish with health. He smelled like cotton candy and French fries. Two of my favorites!

So we were grinning at each other like a couple of idiots, when I remembered I had a mission, and he remembered the same.

"Listen, sorry to be a dick, but visiting hours were over a while ago. But if you want to leave your phone number, I could call you when we're back up for guests."

I laughed at his audacity. T. Starr, R.N., his name tag read. "I'm getting married in a few days, T. Starr," I replied. "But that's the nicest offer I've had all week."

"Nuts!" he said, snapping his fingers. "Guess my horoscope was wrong this morning."

"Stick with the comics," I advised him, then took off my sunglasses. I blinked painfully at the fluorescents, then caught his gaze and said, "I've got special privileges, T. Starr."

"Yup."

"I can come and go no matter how late it is."

"Yep, you sure can."

"Tell the charge nurse, will you?"

"I am the charge nurse."

Finally, a break. "Well, spread the news, T. Starr. Betsy Taylor. Unlimited visiting privileges."

"Yup, you can come and go whenever you want, everybody knows."

"And you have a very nice evening."

"No phone number?" I heard him ask mournfully, and I snickered. Even deep in the thrall of sinister vampire mojo, he was still trying to score. T. Starr was gonna go far.

I pushed open the door to Jessica's room, ignoring the soft sigh of the hydraulic hinges (or whatever made big doors wheeze like that), and stepped inside just in time to hear some pompous asshole say, "—really a very rare form of blood cancer. A fascinating case study, really."

"No thanks," Jessica said. Sighed, really . . . her normally strident tone of voice was running at about 15 percent.

"But if my colleagues could read about your case in *J.A.M.A.*, they might be able to help others with your condition."

I knew from my two-year stint as a medical secretary that *J.A.M.A.* was the *Journal of the American Medical Association*. *J.A.M.A.*, along with the *Lancet*, were two of the biggies for docs to publish the weird and unusual.

"No thanks."

"Really, Miss Watkins, you're being a little selfish, don't you think?"

A doctor couldn't write up a patient without his or her permission.

"Miss Watkins, don't you think?"

But they were supposed to *ask*. Not nag. Not guilt trip.

I opened my mouth to leap to Jessica's rescue, when the bathroom door slammed open and Detective Nick Berry snarled, "The lady said *no*, asshole. Take a walk."

I was actually glad to see him, but had to wonder . . . when did he sleep? Or work? For that matter, how'd he keep getting up here?

"Detective Berry, it would be a pity to ban you from the floor. Your visits seem to have a positive effect on my patient."

"No . . ." Jessica's voice was a thread. I could tell it hurt to talk. "Don't do that . . . maybe I could do the . . . the thing . . ."

"Forget it, baby," Nick told her.

"Yeah," I said. I tried to slam the door behind me, but the damned thing just slid slowly shut on those whispery hinges. "Forget it, baby."

From the way the men jumped (Jessica, obviously, didn't have the strength), I realized they hadn't known I was in the room.

And the dickhead bullying my best friend? When he wasn't flushed red to the eyebrows, he was probably almost normal-looking. Mussed brown hair, cut short. About my height, with bluish-green eyes and a truly heroic nose. Slump-shouldered and too thin for his height. Bony wrists sticking out of the lab coat. A full-on, grown-up geek. And let's not forget about that spectacular blush! I couldn't tell if he was embarrassed or angry. I was hoping for embarrassed.

"Hey, shitstain, ever hear that no means no?"

"What are you people doing here after visiting hours?" B. McGill, M.D., Oncology, sputtered.

"Kicking your ass." I crossed the room in a hurry—Nick had his gun out of his holster, guess I'd startled him, too—and picked B. McGill up. By his throat.

I won't lie. It felt gooooood.

"Don't. Bully. My friend. Ever. Ever! Again." Each word was punctuated by a teeth-rattling shake. B. McGill's eyes were starting to roll like dice.

"Let go, Betsy, he's mine."

"Back off, Nick. I'm *starving*."

"Awwww." Jessica smiled. "I hate it when Mom and Dad fight."

"I can't let you commit felony assault on him, even if he's the biggest dick on the ward."

"Nick? Sweetie? You couldn't stop me with a flamethrower."

"Rrraaggle," B. McGill managed.

"Betsy. There are days when I almost don't hate you, so don't make me shoot you."

"Oh, go ahead and shoot!" I snapped. "The way my week's going? You think I'm scared of your thirty-eight?" And what happened to his Sig? How many guns did the guy have, anyway?

"Kids, kids," Jessica said.

"Gragggle."

"Put him down! Now!"

"Make me."

"Gggkkkk!"

"Kids?"

I heard the click as Nick cocked his gun. I could hear the bullet tumble into the chamber. The barrel looked really big. That was *fine*. Finally, a foe I could grapple with, a problem I could confront head on. *Misplaced aggression*, Sinclair whispered in my head, which was irritating. For an undead (possibly all-the-way dead) runaway groom, he had sure made himself at home in my brain.

"Kids, Dr. McGill is out cold."

I looked. Nick looked. She was right. His head was lolling, and he was drooling on my wrist. Well, shit. That was no fun at all. I dropped him, and he hit the tile and splayed in a most unflattering way. Nick put his gun away.

We glared at each other across Jessica's bed.

"Pull that again, and I *will* arrest you."

"Draw down on me again and I *will* eat you."

"Again," he sneered. He poured Jessica a cup of water and fixed the bed so she was sitting up. He guarded her like a pissed off mama cat, while she drank it all down.

"Oh, like it was such fun for me, too, that first time! Get it through your head, lamebrain, I was a brand-new dead girl! I didn't even know I was a vampire until my teeth came out. I went to you for help, remember?"

"Help?" he nearly shrieked.

"How could I know what chomping you would do?"

"You didn't think biting me on the neck and drinking my blood would be problematic?"

Wince. *Score one for Nick. Never mind.* "In case it's escaped your notice, I'm one of the good guys! I kill bad vampires and stop serial killers and—and—" I was going blank. What other good things had I done? Surely there were at least a few more . . .

"Of course you stop killers, why do you think I've been feeding you information for the last eighteen months? Because I'm soooo in love with you?"

"That was the prevailing theory," I admitted, feeling vain and stupid at the same time. "Of course, I'm revising it rapidly. So you, uh, don't love me, yeah, I'm getting that."

"Not fucking likely, you blond leech on legs. I dream about locking you up in a sunny cell."

Jessica said nothing. And I kept my face perfectly straight. So Nick didn't know everything about me. Thank goodness! He probably thought a cross or holy water would hurt me. Excellent.

"You know something, Nick? I'm glad you don't like me. Because you're a self-absorbed, overreacting, testosterone-filled, gun-toting dipshit."

"Will you two cut the shit?" Jess demanded. "I'm having a real crummy day. Night. Whatever."

"He started it."

"You started it."

"I'm ending it! I will turn this hospital bed around right now if you two don't knock it off. And before you ask, Bets, I didn't clue him in as to what you are."

"Of course you didn't." Jess looked ghastly and had lost more weight. Trouble was, she didn't have that much to lose in the first place. Five pounds from her was, like, 10 percent of her body weight. Or whatever. "Sinclair's mojo wore off. Nick and I already discussed that."

"Yeah," she said. "You know, when I'm out of this bed, we're going to have to find a way for everybody to play nice."

I grimaced. And Nick looked like someone had placed a scorpion on his tongue.

I stepped over the unconscious asshole, gently put a finger on Jessica's chin, looked at her neck, then turned her head and looked at her other side. Then I looked at her wrists.

Clean as a whistle. I'd check her thighs, next (wasn't looking forward to *that* wrestling match), and then her—

"Don't bother," Nick grumped. "I already looked."

"Yeah, and here I thought we were going to get sweaty, and it was just another exam. What are you guys looking for?"

"There's a lot of weird stuff happening all at the same time," I replied. "I thought it was kind of interesting that you had a big-ass relapse around the time everybody started disappearing."

"No bites," Nick told me. "Not even a scratch."

"So this is just bad timing?"

"Luckily for you."

"Oh, put *both* your guns away," I snapped. "Nobody's impressed."

"I am," Jess said cheerfully. "In fact, it's turning me on like you wouldn't believe."

"I'm outta here."

"Wait! You said everybody was disappearing? Who?"

"I'll tell you the whole story after."

"After what?" I heard Nick ask as the door started to wheeze shut behind me.

"After it's all over," Jessica sulked. "She keeps me out of the cool stuff until it's too late to have any fun of my own."

"Humph," Nick replied.

I couldn't believe, all this time, that I thought he'd been on my side! That he'd liked me. Here it was all a lie, he hated my guts and fed me info just to get creeps off the street. Not caring, I assumed, if I got hurt or even killed in the process.

Jeez, he'd made a special trip to my house to tell me all about the serial killer Laura went to town on! He must have known I wouldn't have known about him, avoiding the news as I did.

What a manipulative bastard! He'd been pulling all our strings for so long, I didn't—

Whoa. What?

I wheeled around, marched back to the room, shoved the door open, waited patiently for it to actually *be* open, then rushed in and grabbed Nick's head in my hands before he could turn, much less find his gun.

"Betsy! What the hell do you think you're—"

I ignored her. "Nick."

"Yes."

"You have to tell the truth, Nick."

"Yes, I do."

"Are you responsible for Sinclair's disappearance?"

"I wish."

"Do you know who is?"

"No. But good luck to them."

I thought for a second, never breaking eye contact. "Do you have any advice?"

"Go back to the beginning. Find them. Kill them."

"Go back to the beginning?"

"Who else is gone?"

"Marc. Cathie-the-ghost. Tina. My father and his wife. Antonia. Garrett."

"Then it's personal. You already know who's doing it. Go back to the beginning."

I stared at him thoughtfully. He was dreaming with his eyes open, looking not at me but through me, past me. "I'm sorry for what I did, Nick, and for what I did just now. You'll remember everything . . . in five seconds."

"Great," Jessica snapped. "Leave me to deal with the fallout."

"Sorry, hon. Catch you later."

"Let me guess!" she hollered. Wow, water had certainly perked her up. "After you go back to the beginning!"

Well, yeah.

Chapter 24

What did it mean? I wasn't a detective, God knew. And the people around me usually did the thinking. That was how I liked it. I liked that Tina and Sinclair dealt with most of the shit. I liked that another vampire looked after the other Fiends, that two other vampires looked after my nightclub, Scratch. Shit, Jessica had even hired someone to feed my cat. My time was spent reading, snacking, fucking, wedding planning, playing bartender in the kitchen with my friends, and occasionally vanquishing evil . . . again, with help.

The answering machine in the kitchen was blinking. I scowled at it, then pressed "Play."

"Hi, Betsy. Michael Wyndham. We're coming up empty. Completely cold trail. The Pack members in the area haven't seen either of them. We're still looking. Call me if you find anything."

"Hi, hon. It's Mom. The baby is doing fine. I thought you might want to know. Laura's here, if you need either of us. So . . . talk to you soon?"

My, my. Weren't those two getting thick as thieves?

"Hi, Betsy, it's Marc. Man, I hope you get this. Anyway, call me right away." He left a phone number—not his own cell phone—with an unfamiliar area code.

"Hello, Jessica. It's Don. Listen, I set up that new tax shelter for you, I just need you to sign some paperwork. I can come over to your place whenever you like. We can shelter a good seven figures, and as you say, you'd rather give it to charity than the government. Your wish is this CPA's command. Call me."

Ah, Don Freeman, the sexiest accountant on the planet. When he'd first come to the house (he was always bringing things for Jess to sign, and nobody expected a mega-millionaire to come to them), I'd mistaken him for a Minnesota Viking. Shoulders out to *here*.

"Betsy, why the hell haven't you called me back? It's Marc again. Listen, call me. I'm starting to worry."

He was starting to worry? He sounded fine, not dead at all. And not under duress. I leapt for the phone, played his first message back again, and punched in the number.

"Pirate's Cove Resort, Little Cayman."

"Uh, yeah. I'm looking for Dr. Marc Spangler? He left this number?"

"I think he's still scuba diving."

Scuba diving?

"Can you hold on, while I check?"

"Take your time," I managed through gritted teeth.

There was a clunk as someone put the phone down.

He was on *vacation*! Oh, I would kill him. I'd eat him alive and then cut him into a thousand tiny pieces and then set each piece on fire. Then I'd force the ashes to watch reruns of *Survivor*, Season 4. Then I'd—

"Hello?" Marc panted. "Betsy? Is that you?"

"Sorry to interrupt your scuba-ing," I said coldly.

"Oh, that was this morning. I've been hanging around the bar waiting for you to call back. Listen, I've been trying to reach you for days."

"Yes, I know! What's going on? Are you really in the Bahamas?"

"The Caymans," he corrected, "and yeah. But this is the getaway of all getaways. Cell phones are dicey, and so is their Internet connection. We just had a wicked bad storm come through here, which didn't help. Scuba diving's been for shit ever since."

"But what are you doing there?"

"Boning my brains out," he said, sounding way too cheerful. "You know David Ketterling? The cute new pediatrics fellow?"

I had a vague memory of Marc burbling about the new guy at the hospital, but had paid it no mind at the time, since Marc, as we all knew, had no life beyond . . . well, us.

"Well," he bubbled on, "we both had our four-day stretch at the same time, and his grandma owns this resort, so on the spur of the moment—"

"You left the country with a total stranger."

"It was more romantic in my head," he admitted.

"Marc, I've been worried to *death*!"

"I'm sorry, Betsy. I told you, it was spur of the moment. And I've been trying to call since we got here. David was the one who suggested we use the lodge landlines. I can't believe I didn't think of that three days ago."

"Guess you had other things on your mind."

"And in my mouth," he said cheerfully.

"Thanks for that grotesque little mental image."

"Homophobia rearing its ugly head?"

"Honey, if Jessica was telling me about Nick's body parts in her mouth, I'd have totally the same reaction."

"Hey, is she around? Let me talk to her. David's dad is a king shit oncologist in New York. He had a few ideas."

"Um . . ." The temptation to pour all my troubles over the phone line like smelly oil was almost too much. He could be back here this time tomorrow. I wouldn't be by myself. He was a doctor, he was smart, he was funny, we were good buds. He could help me. He *would* help me.

And the only thing it would cost him would be his first vacation in years. His first romantic getaway in five years.

I opened my mouth. Marc to the rescue!

My mouth wasn't paying attention to my brain, because what came out was, "She's out stocking up on tea and cream. I'll tell her about your new boy-toy, though."

"He's a *man*-toy, and don't you forget it, blondie. Listen, I'll be back on Sunday. How goeth the wedding plans?"

"Wha? Oh. Everything's fine. I found a dress, and of course Sinclair has about forty tuxes already." Two lies and one truth. "Listen, I'm glad you're okay. I was—I was worried."

"Oh, who'd do anything to me? When you'd give 'em the smackdown?"

Who indeed. But at least they couldn't get to you, Marc.

"So I'll see you in a couple of days, okay? Call me at this number if you need anything."

"Oh, please. Everything's fine. Have fun. Give what's-his-face a dry peck on the cheek from me."

"No romance in your soul," he teased. "None at all."

He hung up.

And then it was just me. Again.

Chapter 25

Go back to the beginning.

Whoever was pulling all the crap, they are not afraid of me.

What did it mean? Or was I kidding myself, trying to play detective? Maybe this shit was all random. I mean, I was a vampire. My friends were ghosts, vampires, werewolves, millionaires, ER docs. Why wouldn't weird shit happen all of a sudden? Weird shit *did* happen all of a sudden. Just not to everyone, and not all at once. Usually.

I looked at my watch. Almost eleven o'clock. Too

late to call Mom back. Not that I was in the mood. But the werewolves were probably still up and around.

I punched in Wyndham's cell number, and he picked up immediately.

"Yes, Betsy?"

"How'd you know it was me?"

"Caller ID, dear. What can I do for you? Have you heard from our wayward lambs?"

"No, I was just returning your call. Wait a minute. My name wouldn't show up on your—"

"No, but your landlady's does. And she's in the hospital right now, yes? Unlikely to be phoning me." There was a pause, and then he added, "We did our research, dear."

"You did?" I said, mildly creeped out.

"We've looked into a few more things since our arrival here. It simply will not do to underestimate you again." He laughed, a rich, deep chuckle.

In the background, I could hear, "Is that Betsy? Let me talk to her."

"Stop that, you're married." Then, louder, "Betsy? Are you there?"

"Of course I'm here," I grumbled. "Where the hell else would I be?"

"As I said in my message, the trail is cold. I think you may have to prepare yourself for the worst."

"I've been doing that since I woke up dead," I lied, trying to sound tougher than I felt.

"Uh-huh. But there is a somewhat larger problem we'll have to deal with."

"Fabulous. Hit me."

"The full moon, dear. It's in two days."

"What?"

"The. Full. Moon. We. Will. Get. Hairy."

"Cut that out. Sorry. The werewolf I lived—*live*—with doesn't do that."

"Right. But the rest of us will, except Jeannie, who's human, and Lara, who's too young."

Dimly, I heard, "Come on! Lemmee talk to her."

"Shut up, or I'm calling your wife. Betsy? Are you there?"

"Yes," I said, my patience stretched almost beyond endurance. "So you'll have to leave town?"

"Not at all. We'll stay."

"You think the good people of Minneapolis won't notice werewolves running around on Nicollet Avenue?"

"Give us a little credit, Betsy. In fact, we might be

able to find Antonia and her mate on all fours. Our senses are much, much keener when we run with the moon."

"Well, do that. Run along with the moon. Have fun. Keep me posted."

"I have a favor to ask."

"Of course you do."

"Would it be all right if my wife and cub stayed with you during the first night of the full moon? This is a strange city, and I prefer not to leave them unguarded while my Pack members and I go hunting."

Dimly in the background: "I don't need a damned babysitter, Michael!"

"Uh, maybe you better run that one by the little woman first."

"I will pretend," he chuckled, "you didn't just call her that. May we impose?"

I sighed. *I don't get these people.* "Sure. Be nice to have some company. But Michael?"

"Yes?"

"Tell her to leave the gun at home."

"Well, she'll keep it holstered," he said, sounding almost shocked.

"When should I expect you?"

"Two days, maybe sooner. We'll call before coming by."

"Oh, I can't wait. I'm all atingle," I muttered, hanging up.

Derik was right. Definitely a cultural thing.

Chapter 26

"I think this is a sign from God," my half sister, Laura, told me after she took a sip of her orange pekoe.

I managed not to groan out loud. She'd swung by for tea, showing up about twenty minutes after I woke up (being the queen, I usually woke up around 4:00 p.m. or so, and could go outside without being sautéed).

As usual, she was indecently beautiful: about my height, with long buttercup-blond hair caught up in a sensible ponytail. No makeup. Tan capris and a faded blue oxford shirt. Navy blue Keds, one black sock and one navy blue sock. Big, gorgeous blue eyes framed by lashes that you usually only saw on little boys.

I'd given serious thought to not inviting her to my wedding, because, bottom line, she looked better on her worst day than I did on my best. Fortunately, I quickly came to my senses. Well. Six or seven days later, anyway.

"Really, I think God is trying to tell you something," the daughter of the devil went on. (Have I mentioned? She rebelled against her mother, the Lady of Lies, by being a faithful churchgoer). "You should take it as a sign. I was praying over it just last night."

"Laura, what the hell are you talking about?"

She frowned. "Don't talk like that. I'm saying that perhaps your wedding to the king of the vampires wasn't meant to be. He could have picked any other time to leave you, but he chose now?"

"That's the thing, Laura." I ignored my own tea. I was ragingly, crazily thirsty, and I didn't give a damn. "I don't think he left me. I think someone snatched him."

"But why? Why would someone do that? No, I think you should cancel your wedding and be thankful he didn't decide to pull this nonsense after you'd been married a hundred years. By then, you'd have been emotionally committed."

"Laura, he didn't run out on me. Even Tina agrees."

"Oh, her." Laura waved Sinclair's most loyal friend away with her unmanicured hand. "Another vampire. What do you expect her to say? You're always complaining that she's more loyal to him than you."

That was true, I had confided that to Laura. I never dreamed she'd toss it back in my face, though. And it was getting *real* hard to hold on to my temper. "She's worried about him. So am I."

"She's a vampire. She lies."

"*I'm* a vampire."

"Yes, well. I know you're doing the best you can."

"When you said you wanted to come over to help me figure out what to do, this was your big plan?"

"I'm helping," she said, reaching for my hand. I snatched it away. "You need friends now, Betsy. Besides your mother and a sick Jessica, I'm the only one left who really cares about you."

"Laura. Darling? You're so full of shit your eyes are brown."

She stiffened. "Don't talk like that."

"Then cut the shit. Jeez! Did you really come to my house—"

"Jessica's house."

"—to encourage me to forget about the man I love? Who's either dead or captured? To blow off Tina, who spends all her time trying to make our lives as comfortable and murder-free as she can?"

"God doesn't want you to throw in with the minions of Satan," she sniffed. "Don't ignore the signs."

"What the hell do you know about God, you murdering psychotic spawn of Satan?"

She was on her feet. So was I. "Don't talk to me like that!" she shrilled, our faces only inches apart.

"Or what? You'll give me shitty, insensitive advice?"

"It's not my fault that creature tricked our father, birthed me, then went back to Hell!"

"Well, it's not *my* fault I'm a vampire who fell in love with a vampire!"

"You can control who you live and—and fornicate with. *I* can't control my bloodline."

I felt my eyes bulge. "Are we really playing Who's The Biggest Sinner?"

"You chose to throw your lot in with him," she went on. "I didn't choose what happened to me."

"Oh ho! The prude is rearing her ugly head. It's not the wedding that's bugging you, it's the living in sin."

"It's a sign," she repeated stubbornly. "You're blind not to see it."

A chilling thought occurred to me. "Laura? Honey? Did you snatch my fiancé? Did you stick him with that light-show sword of yours?"

"I did *not*."

"I've seen your temper tantrums before, Laura, so don't get up too high on that horse. People usually die when you get pissed."

"They do not! Not real people, anyway. And you're one to talk, you have to drink blood to keep walking around. You—and your kind—are abominations!"

"At least our socks match!"

"That's it!" She threw up her hands. "I'm leaving. I might have known you would spurn perfectly good advice."

"Spurn this," I said, and gave her the finger.

She looked like she'd found a minnow in her cereal, which was probably close to the expression on my own face. She turned, and I grabbed her shoulder and shoved her across the kitchen. She bounced off the wall, hit the floor, but was back on her feet in half a second. Just in time for me to grab her by the throat and slam her against the wall.

That's when I noticed the bright light just below my left eye. Her sword. She could call it up simply by force of will. It was made of Hellfire, and turned vampires into towers of flame, and then ash. Where it went when she wasn't using it, even she didn't know.

"Let go," she grated.

"Put it away," I snapped back.

"Let *go*."

"Put it *away*."

The light from her sword—if my eyes could have watered, they would have. They would have been streaming by now. As it was, I couldn't see out of that eye at all.

"You're not leaving until you tell me what you did."

"Put me down or I'll—"

"What? Kill me? Like you killed Sinclair?"

"I didn't kill him! I wouldn't do that to you!"

"No, you just suggested I leave him forever."

"For your sake!"

"No, for yours. It's hard to pretend to be Miss Goody Goody of the universe if your sister is the queen of the vampires, isn't it?"

"You know what you're doing is wrong."

"Says the girl with a temper-powered sword."

"I don't mean to lose my temper."

"Did you lose your temper with Sinclair?"

"No!"

"How about Antonia and Garrett? You nearly beat Garrett to death once. Did he piss you off again? Did you dispatch him with your handy-dandy sword, get rid of Antonia, and then lie yourself black in the face?"

"I don't lie!"

Ah. There we go. Her eyes were shifting from blue to poison green. Her blond hair was growing red streaks. She was losing her temper. She wasn't Laura, daughter of a pastor. She was the Devil's Own, and she was in my kitchen with a weapon that could kill me.

Excellent. "Fess up, Red. What'd you do?"

"I did *nothing.* Let me go or I'll—"

"Kill me?"

"Let me go," she hissed. "Let me go or I'll kill you, and never mind if I'm sorry after."

"Are you really going to stick me with that thing? Kill your only sister? Orphan BabyJon . . . twice in one week?"

"All that and more if you don't let me *go* now let me go *let go* of me right now, Vampire Queen, right now!"

"What'd you do, Laura?"

"Let go of me!" she screamed, and behind me, the window over the sink shattered.

"Whoa. New trick. Nice one, devil's daughter. Any other new stuff you want to share with the class?"

She was silent for a long moment, and I suddenly felt silly, hoisting my little sister by the neck a good foot off the ground, trying to avoid the sword pointing at my eye. Was this what happened when things went wrong all at once? You couldn't trust *anybody*?

"I see what you're doing. It won't work. Put me down, please."

Her eyes were blue again, the red fading to blond. The sword disappeared in a flash. No, it didn't work. If she had done something, it likely would have come out when she was her other self, her darker self. When she was in a temper, she lost her mind. She wasn't sly, like her mother. Just red-rage pissed. Too pissed to lie.

But now she was calm again. Careful again. Now she could lie.

I put her down.

"Really, Betsy," she fumed, straightening out her mussed shirt. "What would Jesus do?"

"Turn you into loaves and fishes?"

"I've had about enough of your blasphemy." She started for the door, puffing her bangs out of her face as she stomped past me.

"You're a lot more interesting when you're pissed!" I yelled after her.

"Go to hell! And I mean that as a literal invitation."

"Where do you think I am right now?" I cried, but the slamming of the front door (damn, she must have really booked down that long foyer) was my only answer.

Chapter 27

I didn't want to do it. In fact, I could think of about a thousand things I'd rather do, including having a root canal without anesthesia.

I resisted it as long as I could. Well, I resisted it for about ten minutes after I had the idea. But this could be considered "the beginning."

It was also right around the time Nick would have realized I was a vampire, and that we had stomped all over his brain with big black boots. But Nick wasn't the only one we'd vampire mojoed and regretted it, after.

One phone call to Tina, who was in the middle of trying to cross the border into Switzerland, was all it took. This was a surprise. Not that she had the info. Frankly, I had no idea Switzerland was anywhere near France.

"Isn't that, like, way farther north? Like by Greenland?"

"My queen, how may I be of service?" Tina replied, sounding harassed.

"I need Jon Delk's home address."

Long pause.

"Tina? Stupid cell phones . . ."

"My queen, what good would that information do you? As you have promised not to leave the house until I return."

"Every day is another pint of Sinclair's blood, Tina, assuming he's still alive at all." I could actually feel her wince through the phone. "Delk's old job was killing vampires, and he hates Sinclair more than anyone I know. It's worth paying a visit to the family farm, don't you think?"

Another pause, this one shorter. Then: "Bring Laura."

"Sure," I lied. Damn. I was getting good at lying

through my fangs. I'd make it up to Tina once she got back.

"And please call me the minute you find out anything," Tina was saying. "Or don't find out anything. It's an excellent idea, Majesty. I just wish I was there to run the errand for you."

"You've got your hands full already, sunshine. Now hit me with the address, please."

"I've text messaged it to your phone while we've been talking."

"Sneaky and efficient. That's my girl."

"Majesty, it's kind of you to pretend I'm actually being of assistance."

"Stop that," I ordered. "There's no point in beating yourself up. You had an important job to do, and you did it. Who could have predicted all this?"

"Someone," she said, "my age with my IQ."

"Whoever did this took him out from under my nose. Did all this shit right in front of me, and I didn't even notice. Whatever's happened . . . well, it's on me, that's all. Not you."

"Kind," she replied, "but untrue. Take all care, Majesty. How I adore thee."

"What?"

"N-nothing."

Awkward!

As we hung up, I found myself wondering about the mysterious Tina. How had she turned into a vampire? Who had done it, and why, and where were they now? I had no answers here, only her unabashed devotion. In fact, the only person I knew less about was my recently vamoosed fiancé.

How was it that these two vampires, who seemed to care so much about me, had remained so mysterious about their pasts?

Well, wondering wasn't getting me any closer to finding Sinclair. After some digging (I was always misplacing the damned thing), I found my cell in the bottom of an old Louis Vitton purse Jessica had bought me for my twenty-first birthday.

I noted not only the address but precise directions (I knew Tina would make sure she could track down a Blade Warrior if necessary), and got ready to make the long drive to the Delk family farm.

Chapter 28

Jon Delk's parents lived in a St. Paul suburb, but lately he was spending a lot of time at his grandparents' farm in Burlington, North Dakota. I made the fourteen-hour drive in nine hours, mostly because I didn't have to stop to pee or eat, and because I went ninety on the interstate almost the whole way. I was pulled over three times, all three times by single male state troopers. Didn't get a ticket once.

It was the next evening—I'd had to get a motel room just before sunrise, but was on the move again by 5:00 p.m. the next afternoon.

Long gone were the Minnesota cornfields I was used to; out here, close to the Canadian border, it was all wheat fields and sloughs. Got kind of monotonous after a while. At least cornfields were an interesting color.

I pulled into the mile-long drive and shut off the engine (I'd picked Sinclair's banana yellow Ferrari for this drive . . . ninety felt like fifty), staring at the neat, large cream-colored farmhouse with not a little trepidation. I wasn't at all looking forward to what was coming next.

For one thing, it was late—for farmers, anyway. Ten o'clock at night. For another, Delk and I had not exactly parted on good terms. Specifically, he found out we'd stomped around inside his head and was not at all pleased. He expressed this by shooting me. (It was astonishing how often this sort of thing happened.) Then he'd stomped out, and we hadn't seen him since.

Making him a pretty good suspect for all the weird goings-on.

I stumbled up the gravel driveway, regretting my choice of footwear. I was wearing lavender kitten heels to go with my cream linen shorts and matching cardigan (sure, it was eighty degrees outside, but I felt cold almost constantly).

I went up the well-lit porch steps, inhaling myriad

typical farm odors on my way: manure, wheat, animals, rosebushes, the exhaust from Sinclair's car. There were about a zillion crickets in the back field—or at least, that's what it sounded like.

I knocked on the porch door and was instantly distracted when a shirtless Delk answered.

"Betsy?" he gaped.

Farm Boy was *built*. Too young for me (not yet drinking age), blond, nice shoulders, fabbo six-pack. Tan, really tan. Blond hair almost white from being out in the sun all day. He smelled like soap and healthy young man. His hair was damp from a recent shower.

"What are you doing here?"

"Huh?"

His blue eyes went flinty, and he squinted past me, trying to see past the porch light into the dark driveway. "You didn't bring anyone with you, did you?"

"I came by myself."

"Well, I'm not inviting you in." He crossed his (muscular, tanned) arms across his (ripped, tanned) chest and glared.

I opened the screen door and pushed my way past him, gently. "Old wives' tale," I said. "Got any iced tea?"

Chapter 29

My grandparents are asleep upstairs," he said, keeping the crossbow pointed in my general direction, while I dropped six sugar cubes into my tea. "Twitch in their direction, and I won't take the arrow out."

"I tremble and obey. Got any lemon?"

"Yes, and you can't have any."

"Crybaby." I took a sip, then dropped in two more cubes. Delk knew that a stake (or wooden arrow) to the heart wouldn't kill me like it would any other vampire . . . but until he pulled it out, I'd do an excellent impersonation of a dead girl. "Don't worry, I grabbed a snack on the way." From that pig of a Sleep E-Z Motel front desk guy who'd actually *goosed* me while I signed the register. I'd nearly bitten his fingers off. Settled instead for hauling him behind the registration desk and helping myself to a pint.

Delk shifted in his chair, the arrow point never wavering. "What do you want?"

"Oh, the usual. World peace, a pair of Christian Louboton heels, a perfect wedding."

He tried not to wince, and I pretended not to notice. "Still marrying King Psycho, huh?"

That remains to be seen. Did you kill him, Delk?
"'Fraid so," I replied with a cheerfulness I sure didn't feel.

"What do you want?"

"Info."

"So take a community ed course."

"I don't want to learn how to throw clay, Delk. Some extremely weird things are going on in St. Paul. I was wondering if there was anything you wanted to tell me."

"Why don't you just mind fuck me and get it over with?" he sneered, but the tip of the crossbow shook.

"Why don't you just answer me?" I deliberately looked away. I didn't want to take a chance on even accidentally mojoing him. The poor kid had been screwed over enough by me and mine. "People are getting hurt. Some of them are victims. My dad's dead. My stepmother's dead, and I'm BabyJon's new mommy. Vampires have gone missing, and people are acting weird. Jessica's trying not to barf out all her guts from chemo."

Delk's jaw dropped in what I hoped was unfeigned surprise. "Jesus Christ!"

"Something's going on. And . . . well, I couldn't help wondering."

"You think *I* killed your parents?"

"She wasn't my mother," I said automatically.

"I didn't have anything against your dad and your stepmother. I never even *met* them. And you thought I—"

"Well. You and I didn't exactly part on good terms."

He snorted and leaned back, and the crossbow dipped until it wasn't quite pointing at my chest anymore. "You mean when I found out that I'd written a book about you—*your* Goddamned biography!—and then Sinclair and Tina made me forget all about it, all to protect the precious vampire nation? Except for some reason this book, which I don't remember writing, ended up getting submitted to a publisher and is a fall title? A fall *fiction* title?"

"Well, yeah," I admitted. "But anything sounds bad when you say it like that."

"I take it Sinclair is gone, too?"

"Yeah."

"Well. I didn't do it. I doubt any of us did. The Blade Warriors disbanded."

I giggled, the way I always did when I heard the name of their kiddie club.

"Knock it off. My point is, I haven't talked to any of them since Anya and Tina broke up. You know about that."

"I also know that we were kind of friends once, and then I let Sinclair and Tina do something I knew was wrong, and then we weren't anything."

"Do you blame me?" he asked quietly, setting the crossbow between the sugar bowl and the cream. You had to admire your North Dakota farms . . . good food, sturdy furniture, checkered tablecloths, crossbows.

"No! *Heck*, no. I never blamed you. I'd have done the same thing. Possibly discharging a few firearms before I left town."

He smiled. "Yeah, I bet. But I've been here helping out with the farm since I last saw you. Grandpa has plenty of help for harvest, so I'll probably finish my senior year at the U this fall. I miss the Cities."

"I bet dorm living isn't your cup of crossbow, either."

He laughed and looked about sixteen instead of twenty. "After the shit *I've* seen? And done? I'd probably strangle my roommate before orientation was over."

"Well, we've got plenty of room at the mansion. You're welcome to crash there until you find a place of your own."

He just looked at me. Now it was my turn to shift uncomfortably. "Look," I continued, "I'm not saying it wouldn't be awkward or anything—"

"Awkward?"

"—but bottom line, we fucked you over, and that was wrong. And I let them do it because I've got responsibilities that I didn't have when I was alive. That doesn't make it right. We owe you one. A big one. You can live with us as long as you like."

"I'm sure Sinclair and Tina would love that."

"They owe you a big one, too."

He chuckled and helped himself to a swig of my tea. "Argh! There's less sugar in a Coke. You'd really let me stay with you."

"Sure. Hey, it'd be a pleasant change for me to *invite* a guest to move in. Usually they just . . . move in."

"How do you know I'm not lying? Maybe I got the drop on Sinclair and Tina and threw your dad down the stairs—I'm sorry about your folks, by the way."

"Thanks, but Tina's alive and well, and my dad died in a car accident."

"Maybe I'm just a really really good actor."

"Well. That's why I didn't call. I wanted to talk to you in person. Watch your face. Your eyes."

He swallowed hard. "Oh."

"You're slick, Delk, but I'm the vampire queen."

He fiddled with the yellow tablecloth for a moment, trying not to stare at me. "I think that's the first time I've heard you refer to yourself that way."

"Yeah, well, it's been a super fun week. And by 'super fun' I mean 'horrible and endless.' "

"Well," he said with the air of a person who had suddenly made up his mind, "I don't know about staying with you. But I'll come back with you and help."

Part of me leapt at the idea. And part of me wanted to cover my eyes and groan. I had figured this meeting would go one of three ways.

One: Delk would throw things, aim weapons at my head, chase me away like I was a rabid coyote. Two: Delk would instantly let bygones be bygones and offer to come back and help (more on that in a minute). Three: some weird combination of one and two.

Once again, I was madly tempted to take him up on his offer, and once again, I wasn't going to allow myself the luxury. For one thing, I had *no* idea what was going on or how dangerous things could get. Delk, although adept at killing vampires *with the Blade Warriors backing him up,* was still little more than a kid. For another, it was no secret to me that Delk had a bit of a crush. Leading him on wasn't an option.

Finally, I didn't drive all the way out here to drag him into my troubles. After what we'd done to him, he didn't owe us a thing.

"After what we did to you, you don't owe us a thing."

"I wasn't thinking 'we' and 'us.' I just want to help *you* out."

"Touching, yet mildly creepy. Nothing's changed, Delk. Once I track Sinclair down, I'm still marrying his sorry ass."

"And the rest of him as well, presumably. Look, Betsy, I—I've missed you. And I consider us even."

"Oh. Even as in, 'Hey, you mind fucked me, but then I shot you in the chest, so let's start fresh' even?"

"Anything sounds bad," he teased, "when you put it that way."

"You're sweet," I said, and I meant it. Once upon a time, I'd thought Delk's crush was cute. Now it just made me tired. I made a mental note: once I'd fixed the current disaster, *however* it shook out, I was going to fix Delk up with someone nice.

Laura?

No, no.

Hmmm.

"—no trouble to come back to the Cities with you."

"You're sweet," I said again, "but it's my mess to clean up, not yours. But think about what I said. About this fall." I drained my tea and finished. "Now, if I expect to make some time before the sun comes up, I'd better book. Sorry to barge in on you like this."

"Wait, wait." Delk grabbed a Post-It and scribbled on it, then stuck it to my arm. "That's my cell. Call me and I can be in the Cities in less than a day."

"Thanks," I said, not mentioning that Tina had extensive files on various ways to track him down. I pulled it off my arm and stuck it in my pocket. "I'll treasure it always."

"Say hi to Jessica and Marc for me."

"Sure. Thanks for not staking me the minute I knocked on your door."

"Aww. You're too cute to stake."

All of a sudden I was in a big hurry to leave. I was afraid I'd weaken and tell him to come back with me—I was so tired of being by myself. And I felt guilty about his crush. He'd forgiven me pretty quickly for what I still considered to be an unforgivable act. Was that my fault? I'd never led him on deliberately. I didn't think.

"Want to hear something funny?" he asked, getting up to walk me to the door.

"Absolutely."

"I wrote the publishing house. The one that's publishing *Undead and Unwed*? I pretended to be a reviewer, and they sent me an ARC."

"ARC?"

"Advanced reader's copy. Of my book. It's kind of cute. It's told in first person. You know—you're telling your own story."

Suddenly the front door was about a hundred miles away. Guilt was washing over me like a tsunami. "Oh?" I managed, trying not to gallop the rest of the way to the door.

"Yeah."

"Delk, I'm—"

"I know." He looked at me thoughtfully. I tried not to look at his nipples. "I guess if you're going to be the queen, you have to be the queen."

Whatever that meant. "Yep, that's about right."

"But I hope you'll remember that you were human first, and for a lot longer."

"I try to." Finally, a pure truth. "Every day, I try to. It's sort of what drives the other vampires batshit."

He grinned. "Well then! An even better reason to keep it up."

"Thanks for the tea."

"Thanks for having the courtesy to come and see me yourself."

He held the door open for me. We stood there, fairly awkwardly, while I tried to think of something to say. I didn't dare kiss him, not even a buss on the cheek. Shaking hands seemed kind of overly formal, given all we had been through. Not doing anything at all would be rude.

"Fuck it," I said, and grabbed him and gave him a resounding kiss on each cheek, real smackers. "There. Bye."

"Hey, if it turns out Sinclair is dead—"

"Stop."

"Too soon for jokes?"

"Just a bit." I started down the steps. "Behave yourself. Maybe I'll see you in September."

"More like probably," he said cheerfully. He let the porch door slam behind him and leaned on the railing. "It'd be worth it just to irritate the piss out of your runaway groom."

"You're not staring at my ass as I walk away, are you?"

"Of course I am!"

I grinned in spite of myself and shot him the finger over my right shoulder. He waved as I started the car and put it in gear, and I flashed my high-beams in response.

Cross another suspect off my list. But I felt slightly better for coming. And I made a promise to myself. Two promises. I would fix Delk up, and no matter what it took, I'd make sure he got the credit for *Undead and Unwed*, as well as the royalties.

How? I had no idea. But it was the least I could do.

Chapter 30

l can't believe you're babysitting me."

"Hey, you didn't have to come."

"Uh-huh. Rattling around that mausoleum you live in was a much better plan."

"Mom, can I have some more paper?"

Jeannie and Lara Wyndham and I were back at the bridal shop. Tonight was the first night of the full moon. My wedding was in four days.

Denial? Was that why I was here? Pretending everything was fine and I really was getting married next week? Well, yeah. Besides, if Sinclair did show up (or if I was ever able to figure out where he was), I had no plans to walk down the aisle naked.

Given that I'd been planning my wedding since the seventh grade, it was slightly insane that I'd left the dress for so late. Not only did it have to be The Dress, but at this stage of the game it needed to require few if any alterations.

The florist was taken care of, ditto the reception menu. The justice of the peace was booked—he was a friend of my mom's. The RSVPs had all come in long before Sinclair had disappeared. It was a small civil ceremony, so there'd be no rehearsal. No brides-maids, either, though I'd picked out designer suits for my girlfriends to wear, all Vera Wangs, all jewel colors.

Speaking of jewel colors, Lara was lying on the floor, drawing with Crayola Sparkly Markers. Jeannie was slumped in one of the armchairs, staring at the ceiling. And, what came as a pleasant surprise, she wasn't armed. And I was trying not to remember the last time I'd been at the bridal shop, when things had been almost normal.

"How was your wedding?" I asked, waiting for the clerk to haul out some dresses.

She snorted. "I didn't have one. The day I met

Michael I got knocked up with this one." She nodded at her daughter. "As far as werewolves are concerned, that was the wedding."

"Really?" I was interested in spite of my own problems. "I'm kind of in the same boat. We've got this thing called The Book of the Dead, which foretold—uh—me. And my fiancé, Sinclair. So he always figured we were married, too. Even when I couldn't stand him, he assumed we were hitched."

"Aggravating."

"Say it twice. Anyway, the last thing he wanted was a real wedding with a dress and a caterer and a cake we can't eat."

"Oh. And now he's gone?"

"Yeah."

Jeannie was probably a lousy poker player. I was grateful she was too tactful to suggest Sinclair hadn't been kidnapped. She looked at me, bit her lip, and then went back to staring at the ceiling.

"I hope we get this cleared up sooner rather than later," she fretted, shifting in her seat. Her shoulder-length hair, normally curly, was bordering on frizzy, thanks to the humidity, and she shoved a wad of it behind one ear and crossed her legs. "I haven't seen my son in a week."

"Oh? How many kids do you have?"

"Lara here, and my son, Aaron. He'll be two next month." She sighed. "Obviously this trip was too dangerous for a toddler."

"Uh." I glanced at Lara, reassuring myself she was engrossed and paying no attention. "Not to tell you your business, but I think it's too dangerous for anybody under thirty."

She smiled thinly. "Lara will be the next Pack leader. The more she knows about the world before she has to take over, the better."

"Yeah, but—not much time to just be a kid, huh?"

Jeannie said nothing. But I could tell she didn't like it. *What must it be like*, I wondered, *to be a human in the middle of a bunch of werewolves? In love with your husband and glad enough to have kids with him, but caught up in a society with completely different rules?*

I could so totally relate.

"So even though you have a little boy, Lara will—?"

"The mantle's passed down by birth order, not gender."

"How refreshing!" And I meant it. Men usually got all the breaks.

"Yeah. But I see where you're going with all this. And yeah, I wish I could protect Lara from—well, everything. But a werewolf cub isn't like a human child. Even a half/half, like my daughter. They're bolder than we are, and faster, more pragmatic and . . . well, crueler, in some ways. From the day she was born she was different than any human baby. I swear, she was born without the fear gene."

"Fear is a gene?"

"You want to get into it, blondie?" she demanded, but she was smiling. "Because we'll go, if you want to go."

"Don't call me blondie, fuzzball."

"Mom, you worry too much," Lara said from the floor, drawing what appeared to be a field of upside-down mushrooms on fire.

"That's my prerogative."

"What's—"

"It means that as your mom, I retain the right to worry about you pretty much until the day I die."

"Oh, yay," the kid muttered, then giggled when Jeannie nudged her rump with the toe of her sandal.

"So your husband and his buds are running around on all fours in the middle of St. Paul right about now?"

Jeannie shrugged. This was obviously old stuff to her. I couldn't help but admire her. She'd adjusted to her extreme lifestyle change a lot better than I had. Of course, she'd had a few more years to deal with it.

"I wish *I* was on all fours right now," Lara said.

I looked a question at Jeannie, who replied, "Puberty, usually."

"Oh, *that* sounds like a fun time."

She grinned and opened her mouth, but before she could elaborate . . .

"Ah, Ms. Taylor! So nice to see you again."

"Yeah, hi, uh—"

"Misty, Sherri, and I will be heading out for a quick bite, but you're our only appointment this evening. Christopher is in the back, selecting some gowns we think will superbly suit your height and complexion."

"Superb," I said.

"Mega superb," Jeannie added.

"We've got some lovely things in from Saison Blanche, Nicole Miller, Vera Wang, and Signature."

"Terrific. But you know, time's kind of an issue for me."

"And not wanting to be here is kind of an issue for my mom," Lara added, ignoring another toe-poke from her mother.

"Can't I just go in the back and sort of look around? It'd go a lot faster, don't you think?"

"I'm afraid that's against policy, Ms. Taylor. But we're willing to stay as late as necessary this evening to be sure you find the perfect gown."

Jeannie groaned. I couldn't blame her. If I were in her shoes, I'd probably be bored out of my mind, too. In fact, I was sort of amazed that—

(Beth)

"Sorry, what?"

Jeannie glanced at me. "What?"

"What'd you say?"

"Nothing out loud. But I was thinking all sorts of nasty things." She grinned. "What? Vampires can read minds?"

"No." Not entirely true. I could read Sinclair's mind when we were making love. In fact, it was just as well we were fated to rule for a thousand years, because he had *ruined* sex for me with anybody else.

Wait a minute! The Book of the Dead *said* we were fated to rule for a thousand years. There wasn't anything in there about Sinclair being killed before we even got officially hitched.

Why hadn't I thought of that before?

I was so excited I wanted to run out of the bridal shop and—and—well, I wasn't sure what I wanted to do, but I sure didn't want to sit there a moment longer. I—

"Here we are, Ms. Taylor." Christopher emerged from a side hall, where I knew he'd hung three or four gowns in a dressing room for me to try on. It was good timing, since the other three clerks had just left.

Concealing my excitement, I slowly got to my feet, sauntered over to Christopher, gripped him by the elbow, and murmured, "Take us to *all* the dresses."

He wheeled around like a reprogrammed robot and started marching toward the back. Snickering, Jeannie rose and followed, and Lara followed her.

Now we were getting somewhere. That's right, everything was coming up Betsy!

Chapter 31

The salon had, at rough count, three thousand gowns in the back. I could eliminate some right off the bat. No meringue dresses. Nothing with too many beads—I hated shiny. Nothing strapless—I'd freeze my ass off. Nothing with a long train—I'd trip and make a fool of myself, guaranteed. No mermaid styles—the clingy gown that flared out from the knees.

And none of that new slutty style, either—the kind that looked like a traditional dress from the back, but from the front the skirt split just below crotch level and showed miles of leg. Not that my legs weren't fabulous. But this was a wedding . . . some decorum was called for.

I was looking for a nice, creamy ivory. Pure white was too harsh with my undead complexion. Even off-white was a little too much.

Lara went back to coloring, and Jeannie paced around the back like a caged cat. I would occasionally emerge for a thumbs-up or -down.

"No."

"Uh-uh," Lara said, glancing up from her new drawing.

"Doesn't suit you," Jeannie said when I emerged again.

"Mom's right."

And again . . . "Nope."

"Too billowy."

And again. "Your tits are just about popping out. Now, if that's the look you're going for . . ."

And again. "You're lost in all those ruffles."

"Buried," Lara agreed.

"What about some color?" Jeannie asked. Her voice was muffled, as she was pretty far in the back.

"No, I want traditional, yet fabulous."

"I don't mean all red or all blue. But how about

this?" Jeannie emerged holding a cream-colored gown with a plunging-yet-not-slutty bodice, cap sleeves, an A-line style with a simple skirt that fell straight to the floor. Small red silk stars and flowers were embroidered all over the skirt and bodice.

I stared. Lara stared. Then Jeannie looked at the price tag and stared. "Fuck a duck," she said. "Never mind."

"Hold it!"

And that's how the alpha female of the Wyndham werewolves found my wedding gown.

Chapter 32

I t fit you perfectly." Jeannie still couldn't get over it. We had just gotten back to the mansion. "Didn't you say you're getting married in a few days? You really lucked out. Whoever heard of an off-the-rack wedding dress that didn't need alterations?"

"Proof that it's The Gown For Me. Thanks again. If you hadn't found it, I never would have thought to ask for such a thing."

"No need to thank me, my motives were purely selfish. That's three hours of my life I didn't have to waste in that taffeta hellhole. Lara, go find your bag and get ready for bed." She turned to me. "We grabbed one of the bedrooms on the third floor, is that all right?"

"Sure. There's plenty of room up there." I glanced at my watch. Nine o'clock. I was giving serious thought to flipping through the Book of the Dead. But I was also afraid. The last time I'd tried such a stunt, I'd turned into a truly awful bitch for the better part of the evening. Hurt my friends. Hurt Sinclair. It had taken me a long, long time to forgive myself.

And there was Jeannie and Lara to think about. Michael hadn't left them in my care so I could attack them after reading the wrong chapter in the vampire bible.

Worse: the Book didn't have an index, or even a table of contents. There was no way to look anything up. I'd have to flip through it—skim as much as possible—and hope I stumbled across something helpful.

On the upside? The Book was never wrong. It had successfully predicted me, Sinclair, my powers, and come to think of it—

"My baby," I said out loud, ignoring Jeannie's curious look. How did it go? "And the Queene shalt noe a living childe, and he shalt be hers by a living man." Yeah. That was more or less it. When Sinclair had told me at the time, it had depressed the hell out of him. He assumed it meant I'd get knocked up by someone else. But I "knew" a living child who was mine by another man . . . my father.

So the Book of the Dead had been right about a baby. It also foretold that Sinclair and I were supposed to be the king and queen for a thousand years. Did that mean I could quit worrying? That everything would work itself out?

(Beth)

"What?"

"Betsy?"

"What?"

"Your purse is ringing."

I glanced at the table where we habitually tossed our purses, wallets, and keys. Jeannie was right. My purse *was* ringing. I opened it and grabbed my cell.

"Hello?"

"Hey, it's me. Whoa, you actually answered your cell!"

"Hi, Jess, and yes I did. What's up?"

"I was wondering how the dress shopping went."

"Awesomely."

"I'm pretty sure that's not a word."

"Who cares? I found it."

"Great! It's still cream, right? You stayed away from the pure whites?"

"Yeah, and—"

"Great. Come on over to the hospital, will you? I've got something for you."

"You mean right now?"

"No, I mean next month. Yeah, now."

I glanced at my guests, who I assumed were more interested in going to bed than running around the oncology ward at this hour. I covered the bottom half of the phone. "Do you guys mind if I run out for a bit?"

"No," Jeannie yawned. Lara was already sleepwalking toward the stairs, a toothbrush clenched in one fist.

"Okay, Jess," I said. "I'll be there in twenty minutes."

If this is an ambush so Nick can shoot me in the head," I announced, walking into her room, "I'm going to be very upset."

"He went home to crash in a proper bed for a

couple of hours. I practically had to call Security to get him out of here."

"Well. He's worried about you, the fascist."

"He'll get over this latest, uh, wrinkle." Jessica didn't look—or sound—at all sure of herself. In fact, she looked generally ghastly. The new round of chemo was not being kind. And as I'd said, Jessica couldn't afford to lose any weight. But she was smiling and had an expression on her face I knew well: Jessica had a secret.

"You mean the whole mind-rape thing? He *hates* me. And Sinclair."

Jess didn't bother denying it; we'd been friends for too long to take refuge in false comfort. "But he loves me. We'll figure something out. First things first. I've got your wedding present."

She opened the drawer to her right and took out a shoe box wrapped in heavy white paper and topped with a pale blue bow.

I smiled in anticipation. Jessica was rich and had great taste. Even better, she knew what I liked. I plucked off the bow and stuck it to her forehead, ripped off the gorgeous paper, and flipped the lid off the box.

And stared. Inside the box were a pair of Filippa Scott Rosie bridal shoes in the exact shade of my dress (the cream-colored part, that was). I knew she hadn't bought them for less than four hundred bucks. I also knew they were handmade with duchesse satin, with a padded foot bed that meant even with three-inch heels, they'd be comfortable. And the slim bow across the front was just the right touch.

"Oh my God," I said.

"I know," Jessica said smugly, reclining in her hospital bed like a goddess being fed grapes.

"They're perfect."

"I know."

I burst into tears.

"Whoa. Hey!" Jess shot upright, then gagged, and for a minute I thought she'd barf on me while I wept into the shoe box. We both struggled to control ourselves, but only Jessica won the battle. "This really wasn't the reaction I was going for."

I cried harder.

"Betsy, what's wrong? Is it Nick? We'll figure something out. We're going to have to. But I don't think he'd really try to hurt you."

"It's Nick," I sobbed, hiding my face with the box. "It's everything."

"What everything?"

So I told her.

Chapter 33

ow."

"I know," I sniffed.

"Wow."

"I know."

"Why didn't you—never mind. I know why you didn't say anything." She propped her chin in her palm and stared past me. "This stinks to high heaven."

"Yeah. I don't know what to do."

"Well, he's *not* dead." She said this with such authority that I instantly cheered up. "No chance. *No* chance."

"Why? He's not immortal."

"Why? Because he's Sink-Lair, that's why! You think he's easy to kill? You think you wouldn't *know* if your king was dead? He's stuck somewhere. Some asshole snatched him, and you've gotta figure out who."

"That's what I've been trying to do."

"Yeah, so you said. It's not the werewolves, it's not Delk. It's not Laura. It's—what did you say Nick told you? To go back to the beginning?"

"Yeah."

"So when did things start to get weird?"

I thought about it. I took my time, and Jessica let me. It wasn't the fight we'd had over the wedding announcements. Sinclair and I fought all the time. What was the first really weird thing to—

"The double funeral," I said at last. "That's when I realized things were mondo-bizarro. It was like one day everything was the way it's been the last couple of years, and the next, I was alone. You were sick. Dad and the Ant were dead. Tina was in Europe. Mark had disappeared. Laura and Mom blew off the funeral. Antonia and Garrett had vamoosed."

"You think your dad and the Ant weren't killed by accident?"

"Who'd want to get rid of them? I've been so busy

I haven't had time to feel sad. If someone was trying to hurt me, that's not really the way to do it. I guess that makes me a bad daughter, but—"

"But your dad was a pud," Jessica said bluntly, "and that's the end of it."

"I'm wondering if there might be some answers in the Book of the—"

"You stay away from that thing," she ordered. "You going psycho-bitch isn't going to help anything."

I sighed and slumped back. "I suppose."

"Tina called it right. This whole thing reeks like last week's sushi. I wish you would have told me earlier."

"You've got more important things to worry about."

"Oh, what's more important than my best friend?" she asked irritably.

"Your life," I replied. "Focus on getting better."

"Well, today was the last day of chemo. So I ought to be able to come to the wedding without heaving all over my suit. If I have to be dragged in on a stretcher and propped up like Hannibal Lecter, I'll be there," she vowed.

"Revolting," I said. "Yet comforting."

Chapter 34

$\mathcal{l}$ dragged myself into the silent house. The third floor was dark; I assumed Lara and Jeannie had hit the sheets. But this wasn't the week to make assumptions, so I tiptoed up to the third floor and found them in the second bedroom I checked. They were both conked and both snoring. I shut the door and snuck back downstairs.

I kicked off my pumps, tossed my keys in the general direction of the foyer table, then went into the library and sat down across from the Book of the Dead.

The nasty thing was on a mahogany book stand by

the fireplace, open to God knew what page. I stared at it and tried to make a decision. *Any* decision.

"You might as well," a horrifyingly familiar voice said from across the room. "You can't screw this up any worse."

I looked over, and there she was: Laura's mother, the devil, seated behind the desk.

"Fabulous," I muttered.

"So nice to see you, too, dear." Satan looked a lot like Lena Olin: long brown hair streaked with silver. Calm expression, beautiful gray suit, classic gold earrings (in the shape of angel wings!), black stockings, and . . . I peeked under the desk. And groaned silently. She was wearing fourteen-thousand-dollar Manolo Blahnik black alligator boots. "Like them?" She rotated her left foot around her ankle. "I'm sure we could work something out."

"Get lost."

"Now, Betsy. You need me. After all, you're not using that teeny, tiny brain of yours. In fact, you haven't been since this whole thing started."

"And what do you know about it? Scratch that: go away." I wasn't the brightest bulb in the chandelier, but I knew that the devil never gave up anything for free. I was crazy even to be talking to her.

"Oh, Betsy. Don't you know? I can help you. I *want* to help you. Him?" She jerked a thumb toward the ceiling. "Not so much. You think He cares about you now that you're a vampire?"

"I think you lie like old people fart."

"I've never lied to *you*, dear."

I had to admit that was true. Not that I was going to say so out loud.

"It distresses me to see my daughter's sister so upset. So alone in the world. Beset from all sides."

"Really."

"I'll help you, dear. All you need do is ask."

"How about if I ask you to toddle off back to Hell?"

Lena Olin made a *tt'tt!* noise and shook her head sorrowfully, as if at a disobedient daughter. "Why make things so much more difficult? You know I can help you."

"I know nothing's free with you, Lena Olin."

"Let me help you. I'm *dying* to help you. He's still alive, you know. It's not too late . . . yet."

That hurt. A lot. I closed my eyes and chewed on my tongue so I wouldn't say something that would cost me my soul.

"I'll be glad to lend a hand. Because once you have your lover back, you'll stop thinking the worst of my poor Laura. I dislike it when the two of you argue."

I grunted.

"All you need to do is ignore Him and pray to me."

I nearly fell out of my chair. "Pray to *you*?"

"Well, why not? You've seen the state of His world, right?" she said with a gesture. "Your best friend fighting for her life? Your father dead in a senseless accident? Your brother orphaned? You alone in your time of greatest need? And let's not even talk about all the children He does away with every hour of every day. Who knows how long BabyJon has under His regime? Pray to *me*, dear. At least I'm not crazy."

"That's tempting," I said. "Really tempting."

She smiled and smoothed her hair. "We try."

"Well, try this. Take your satanic, designer-shoe-wearing ass right out the door, willya?"

The devil frowned. "Betsy, this is a chance that may never come again."

"Bullshit! You show up whenever I'm in a jam, but

I'm not dumb enough to think you care about me. You're *the devil*, for crying out loud! Your reputation is *horrible*! Now get lost!"

She stood. It seemed to take a long time. It seemed like she was ten feet tall. "Enjoy the funerals, dear. Because without my help, there will be more. And say hello to my dear one when you see her again."

I opened my mouth to say something snappy, but I was alone in the room.

Chapter 35

It took me about ten minutes to stop shaking. It had never been so hard to tell Lena no. Sure, my soul would sizzle in the bowels of Hell for eternity, but on the other hand, I was going to live for at least another thousand years. I wouldn't have to worry about Hell for a long time.

And I believed her when she said she could help me. She wouldn't have shown up here if she couldn't help me. Even now, I was tempted to yell for her, call her back, make a deal . . .

Had she said *funerals*, as in plural?

The desk extension rang, and I nearly jumped out the window. What now? I snatched up the receiver. "Hello?"

"Betsy? It's Mom."

"Hi, Mom. You're up late."

"BabyJon had a late nap," she said ruefully. "But I don't have anything scheduled for tomorrow, so we can sleep late."

"That's good."

"So . . . how are you?"

"Not so good," I admitted. "Things are kind of a mess." *And I deeply, deeply covet Satan's footwear.*

"I'm sorry," she said at once. "I can relate to what you're saying, hon, make no mistake. Do you believe the funeral announcement didn't come out until yesterday? I could have sworn I made the newspaper's deadline, but they said I missed it by twenty-four hours."

"What? You mean Dad and the Ant's funeral?"

"Isn't that stupid? My point is, I've been a bit of a scatterbrain since the accident. And I know I made things harder for you at exactly the wrong time. My only excuse is . . . I don't really know. It's not like I was still in love with your father. I guess I wasn't ready to say good-bye forever. Not so soon after *you* died, anyway."

"I didn't think about it that way," I said. "I guess I shouldn't have been such a jerk."

"Your father died, dear. You were entitled."

"Well, I wasn't there by myself. So how did Dad's coworkers know to be there?"

"Oh, I'd called your dad's secretary—Lorraine?—the day I heard about the accident. And I guess she called the others. And you know your stepmother wasn't averse to using Lorraine for her charity work. That's how her friends knew to come. And of course, I had called you myself."

"Yeah, I remember." Something was bumping my brain like a minnow nudging a weed. It was great that my mom had called, great that she had apologized, great that we were patching things up. Why, then, did I feel so weird? Sort of sick to my stomach and excited at the same time? I was filled with a kind of happy dread, if there was such a thing.

"I thought I'd bring the baby to see Jessica tomorrow," Mom was saying.

I barely heard her. *Start at the beginning. The funeral was the beginning. There was no announcement. So the only people there, would have been people who* knew . . . *who knew . . .*

"I'll visit during afternoon hours if you'd like to join us . . ."

"MARJORIE!" I shouted and heard the receiver crunch as I squeezed it too hard.

Chapter 36

Jeannie and Lara were still conked, and thank goodness. With zero traffic and a lead foot, I made it to the Minneapolis warehouse district in record time, my knuckles white on the steering wheel. I had to be very careful not to bend it out of shape, or even pull it off.

It had been so thoughtful of Marjorie to pay her respects at my father's funeral. Marjorie, in fact, seemed to enjoy being helpful in all sorts of ways. Marjorie, the eight-hundred-year-old vampire who disdained politics.

Why had she come? To see how I was bearing up under all the pressure she was bringing? To try to get a whiff of my pain? To throw me off her scent?

I didn't know. But I was going to find out.

I pulled up outside a dilapidated warehouse, which I knew was beautiful and spacious inside, filled with thousands of books and state-of-the-art computers. Marjorie's digs. Her lair. *Fucking she-spider.*

I didn't bother knocking, just shoved the big double doors open and stomped inside. Like all important confrontations in my life, this one was anticlimactic. Marjorie was nowhere to be found.

The place looked the way it usually did . . . lots of low lighting, comfortable chairs, benches. Lots of conference tables and chairs. Row after row of computers. Quiet as a grave (really!), and smelling like reams and reams of old paper. Oh, and dust. And Pledge!

Well, a case of Pledge wasn't going to stop *me*. It wasn't even going to slow me down. I'd—

(Elizabeth)

"Eric?" I whispered. That tiny voice in the back of my brain, previously so faint I couldn't make out who it was, or even what it was saying, was now quite a bit clearer.

I sniffed. Stupid Lemon Pledge, I wasn't getting anything but—I sniffed harder. Ah! There we go. Yep. Sinclair had been here. Was maybe still here. I stiffened like an English setter on point, then followed the scent through several doorways and down two flights of stairs into a dank basement.

My heels didn't make a sound on the carpeted stairs, which was fine with me, as I was busy trying to look in fifteen directions at once. Had Sinclair really been one town over the entire time? And where was she keeping him, that I could barely hear him? What had she done to him?

The place didn't *look* like a torture chamber. It looked like what it was: an old library, well-maintained, with plenty of money for books and computers. Heck, plenty of money for fluorescent lights as opposed to, say, torches sticking out of the wall.

I finished with the stairs and slid open the huge door in front of me—down there, at least, the place looked like a warehouse. The door rattled past me, and the smell of mildew and sweat assaulted my delicate, queenish nostrils.

The first thing I saw was Antonia in a spacious cage, the kind they used to cage Dr. Lector in *The Si-*

236

lence of the Lambs. She was shaking the bars, and I remembered how claustrophobic she was. Her dark hair was matted with sweat, and her face was pale; she stank to high heaven, and her clothes were filthy. Her big eyes rolled toward me, like an animal in a killing pen, and she greeted me with a shrieked, "Get me *out!*"

Then I saw the coffins. Two of them, chained shut and draped with . . . were those *rosaries*? Yes. Dozens, covering almost every inch of the top of the coffins.

(Elizabeth)

I ran to the one nearest me and stripped the rosaries away, then yanked at the chains until they tore and bent in my hands. I didn't know how Marjorie had placed them—wearing asbestos gloves, maybe? I didn't care. I just had to get him out and face whatever hunger and crosses had done to him.

"Me first, me first, me firrrrsssssstttt!"

I flipped the top off the coffin and bit back a scream. Sinclair, yes. Incredibly wizened, incredibly old. Shrunken. Dried out. His lips were drawn back so his fangs were prominent. He looked a thousand years old. He looked dead.

"Oh my God!" I cried. "Oh, Sinclair! Tell me what to do! How can I—"

"Did your mother never teach you to call before dropping by? Oh, I'm prepared to validate your parking whenever you wish. How clever of you to park right out in the open like that."

I spun so fast I nearly went sprawling. Marjorie was descending the last of the steps; I'd been so caught up in freeing Sinclair I'd never heard her.

"You *cunt*."

"You infant."

"Why?" I had to yell to be heard over Antonia's howls of rage. She was unusually bitchy during the full moon during the best of times . . . which this certainly was not. "Why did you do this?"

"You made it necessary."

I wanted to cry. I wanted to scream. I wanted to punch her sly face in. "What the hell does that even mean?"

She stepped into the room, looking neat and trim in her tweed suit and sensible shoes. "He can't keep you in line. Case in point, your monthly newspaper column. Your autobiography, the fall fiction offering! You live your life openly—everyone around you knows your true nature. You collect people instead of living a solitary life. This is incredibly dangerous, to all you claim to rule. You left me no choice."

"You don't agree with the way I live my life, and so you do *this*?"

"As I said, you forced me to."

"Oh, right. Kidnapping, false imprisonment, torture. Blame *me*."

She shrugged. "Unlike you, I do what must be done. Unlike him, I'm not besotted with your dubious charms. By keeping Sinclair under my control, I'll be able to keep you under control. Because someone has to take charge. And you clearly aren't up to it."

"But—but—"

"I have him. I'll keep him. And I'll kill him the moment you don't do as I say."

"But *I* am the queen!"

"You're a fluke. An accident. And now, you'll be my tool."

She followed my glance into the open coffin. Sinclair was still doing his impersonation of a wizened mummy. "I knew he wouldn't go along with my idea. So I needed him to come and see me. He brought

these two—unexpected, but I could deal with them."
She glared at Antonia, who was making an ungodly
amount of noise rattling her bars.

"But why would he come see you so quickly?"

Her eyes narrowed. "Because I had information for
him. Information is power; libraries are full of power.
I can change records, reveal deaths, make up new
ones, transfer ownership. I can change the facts,
change history, if I like. I can grow my own power
base and even presume to be queen myself someday, if
I like. Eventually, I can discard you on the rubbish
heap of rumor and misinformation. Betsy Taylor was
no queen—she was a pretender, or a prophet, or whatever I'd like to make her. Who, exactly, will dispute
the facts with me? The only vampires old enough to
know better are in Europe. Would they argue if you
die? If Sinclair did?"

I was trying to follow all this. "What information
did you tell him you had?"

"I told him your engagement ring was cursed."

"And he *fell* for that?"

"Of course. Because it is."

"Aw, say it isn't so." I examined my diamond and
ruby ring. "Cursed how?"

"Did you ever read *The Monkey's Paw?*"

"In high school."

"What a pleasant surprise. Here I thought I'd have to show you the picture book. Well, as in that story, your ring grants wishes. But always at a cost. You see, the stones were stolen from an Egyptian tomb. They followed quite a path before they got to me. I split them up and spread their pieces around the world. For research purposes.

"One actually made it back to me here years ago, set in a beautiful antique ring. I buried it far enough away where it couldn't hurt me, but where I could still find it if I thought it might come in handy. And so it did, when Sinclair actually came to me a few months ago and asked me if I knew of any special jewelry he could give you for engagement purposes!" She laughed. "He actually paid me a quarter of a million dollars for it. I couldn't wait to see what you wished for."

A thousand thoughts were whirling through my brain. The zombie, who showed up without explanation three months ago. Tina and Sinclair had tried, and failed, to figure out why it had come. They hadn't even known zombies existed. A total mystery, unsolved until now. But hadn't I wished for a real challenge when the Europeans were in town? A way to prove to myself that I was worthy of my title?

I had wished for everyone to go away and leave me alone—I had never felt more isolated than this past week.

And I had wished for a baby of my own. And then my father . . . and the Ant . . .

"Oh God," I moaned. I was fairly certain I was going to pass out. *I* had killed my father! *My father!* (And the Ant.)

"So, seeing the new opportunity the ring afforded, I then breathlessly contacted the king and told him I had done more research on the stones and found out unpleasant facts. Naturally he came on the run." She frowned at the other coffin. "With company."

I figured Antonia must have had a last-minute psychic flash and either accompanied Sinclair, or followed him. And Garrett had followed her. What a cluster-fuck.

"Apparently she tried to talk him out of coming, but of course Sinclair is sensitive to vampire courtesy, and my great age. And came anyway. And so here we are."

"You bitch."

"Yes, yes. Now. Let's discuss my first orders to you."

I dove at her. Well, the wall, as she neatly side-stepped. "Don't be tiresome," she snapped. "You won't best me. Sinclair is incapacitated, and without him by your side, you are a nothing. A typo. No one has been able to harm me for over five hundred years. You—ow."

I had punched her in the back and felt her ribs splinter. But fast as a snake, she'd gotten a grip on my arm and thrown me into the wall. I felt my nose break as it made brisk contact with the concrete.

I spun and slapped her so hard she staggered side-ways, and I managed to avoid her elbow. I was going to kill this bitch *twice*. Not because she was a duplici-tous cow. Not because she was trying to hurt and ma-nipulate me. I was going to kill her for what she had done to him.

I heard a crunch as my knee broke, and I hobbled sideways, swiping at her with my good leg. With a grunt she went down, but before I could blink she was back on her feet, hoisting her sensible librarian skirt up and kicking me in the same knee that was still try-ing to grow back.

I shrieked and flung myself at her. I was bigger and managed to force her to the floor, then shrieked louder as her fist explored my spleen. I rolled away, fairly certain I was going to puke, then felt her on my back as she slammed my head against the wall.

"This is foolish," she said in my ear. "All you need do is fall in line, and we can get down to the business of governing the vampire nation properly."

I whipped my head back, smiling at the crunch of her nose breaking. I jerked an elbow back, but only caught air. I felt her hands on me, and she pushed, hard. My teeth broke as I hit the concrete again.

Hmm. Getting the shit kicked out of me was no fun at all. I bit back a howl as she twisted an arm so hard, it broke in two places.

(Elizabeth, get away.)

Shut up, Sinclair. I turned just in time to catch a librarian fist in the face, and there went more teeth. I coughed up blood and spat it right in her face.

"Oh, dear! Not . . . *blood*." She laughed at me and licked her lips, her fangs appearing like needles springing from her gums. I slapped her again, and she shook it off, then punched me in the gut. I bent, gagging, and she grabbed my head and twisted.

I just managed to get an arm up before she broke my neck, and we moved around the basement in a flailing dance. Then she stomped on my foot with her sensible soles, and I felt a few more bones break and lost my balance. I went down, and she was right on top of me.

She had both hands around my neck and was squeezing and yanking my head up and down. The squeezing didn't bother me so much (I didn't need the breath) but every time she slammed my head into the floor I heard another fracture. It sounded like someone was crunching ice in my ear. It hurt, *and* it was annoying.

Slam. Slam. Slam. I brought my legs up to wrap them around her neck, but she simply leaned forward and fractured my skull again. And things were getting a little dark in here. I didn't think it was the ambiance. Nope, she was killing me. I'd been stumbling around like an idiot since Sinclair disappeared, had the clue in front of me the whole time

(Go back to the beginning.)

finally figured out who the bad guy was, and for my trouble? She was kicking my ass sideways. It hurt like hell and was fairly humiliating.

"And to think—I thought—you'd be—reasonable." Bitch wasn't even out of breath! Each pause was punctuated by another head slam. I was getting killed by a scrawny suit-wearing woman with graying hair. And sensible shoes!

Black roses were blooming in front of my eyes, and all of a sudden things hurt less. Hmm. Stakes hadn't killed me, and neither had bullets. But if an older vampire did enough damage (particularly to my head), if an older vampire pretty much tore my freaking head off, it seemed that would do the trick. Fine way to find out.

It was all right, though. It really was. I'd been floundering around in the dark for so long, it seemed appropriate that things were going dark for real. She was right; I was no queen. Look how easy she'd led me by the nose, and for how long. Heck, she'd been able to fool Sinclair!

(Elizabeth, get away. Run!)

Easy for *him* to say; he was napping in a nice comfy coffin.

No, it was probably for the best. My dad was dead, practically by my own hand. I'd probably have screwed up BabyJon beyond repair. Antonia had apparently gone completely nuts from the stress of being locked up most of the week. God knew what state poor Garrett was in. Jessica was a goner—you only had to look at the weight dropping off her to see it. And Sinclair—

If this bitch killed me, he was dead meat.

If this bitch killed me, there was no stopping her from hurting anyone she liked. My family. My friends. Sinclair.

The back of my head was sticky with blood; it was running down my face. I had a hundred broken bones; three of my ribs were gone. Not broken. Gone. Blood was draining from me. I had never been so . . .

hungry?

. . . in my life. Never. I needed to drink, and I couldn't. I needed to live, and I wouldn't. But Marjorie had power and energy to spare; the most I'd been able to inflict on her were defense wounds.

Marjorie had power and energy to spare.

Marjorie.

I reached for her. Not with my hands. Not with my teeth. With my mind. Even as everything faded to black I could sense her energy, her strength, and I grabbed for it like a fat kid grabbed for pie. And just like a fat kid, my chubby mental fingers crushed her tinfoil skin, and my chubby mental eyes gleamed at the crumbling, steaming crust.

"*Unh,*" I heard her grunt. She let go of me, her head tossing in confusion. Something had a hold of her and wasn't letting go. I rolled over to see who it was.

There was no one else there. But that didn't matter, because just seeing her like this was making me feel a bit stronger. The black blooms vanished, and I could see again. Her limbs thrashed as the chubby, pie-loving child inside of me poked at her to see what kind of fruit filling was inside.

Mmmmm. Blood pie.

Without touching her, I began to drink.

She screamed and fell to her knees.

No one else is doing it, I realized with more alacrity as the blood rushed into my system. *Just the Queen. The Queen of the Fucking Vampires. Her Queen. And her Queen requires her goddamn, fucking obedience. She has something, I need it, it's mine.*

Mine!

The darling pie-loving child was gone now. I split her open with my mind, grabbed for her, and pulled *everything* she had into me.

Her suit emptied—the blood first, then the shriveling muscles, then the flaying bits of dried skin, and then the billions of splinters of bone.

By the time I was done, I was standing tall over a librarian's suit, a librarian's sensible shoes, and about twenty grams of dust. I felt absolutely fine.

In fact, I had never felt fucking better in my life.

Chapter 37

Power slammed through me, and I screamed. Well, not so much screamed as roared. I felt energy running through my spine like a waterfall; the overload of *good* was becoming worse than the beating. I staggered away from Marjorie's remains and nearly fell into Sinclair's coffin. I grabbed him and *poured* some of the new strength I had into him; it was either get rid of it or blow up.

Even as he stirred, grew younger, grew strong, sat up, it wasn't enough, I was still going to blow.

I stumbled away from Sinclair, kicked Marjorie's

things (and probably a bit of old Marjorie, too, poor thing) out of the way, and reached for Antonia through the bars and *poured* more of it into her.

I was not entirely sure what I was doing and yet wasn't even shocked when Antonia screamed again, a scream that turned into a howl. She dropped to all fours, sprouted dark brown fur, and then an enraged werewolf was howling at the ceiling and tearing at the bars with her teeth.

No fair! I thought. *You're not supposed to be allowed to do that. Rule breaker!*

"Elizabeth!" Someone was shaking me. "Elizabeth! Whatever you're doing, *stop it!* It's too much, you're—"

Through blurred vision I saw Antonia-the-wolf tear through the bars with her teeth and wondered vaguely what the hell a werewolf's teeth were made of. *Titanium?* In no time at all she'd torn or pulled a big enough hole through the bars and wormed through, then attacked the other coffin with desperate savagery. The rosaries flew off, and she started to rip at the chains.

Getting some of my mind back, I began to help her. Well, by began I mean I flipped the coffin lid open as though the chains weren't there, stuck my hands inside, and poured everything I had onto the shriveled thing inside.

In a few seconds, Garrett was sitting up and looking around.

"Wow, I feel terrific! Um. What the hell just happened?" he asked, sounding quite un-Garrett-like.

Whoever had tried to shake me before—that would be Sinclair, right? Sure, I could see him now, it was Sinclair.

Hey, he looks good! I made him all right. That's nice. Now if I could just do something about this force inside of me that feels like it wants to split my skin . . .

"Elizabeth!" His eyes were wide with awe and fear. "Elizabeth, what are you doing?"

And I was still burning up, still exploding, there was still too much of whatever I had taken from Marjorie in me, on me, all over me, around me.

I had an idea, but I knew I only had a few moments of conscious thought left. So I leaned into Sinclair, making him wince with the touch, and whispered my instructions into his ear.

He nodded. "Yes, my Queen."

"Hurry," I finished, and then I collapsed to the ground, wreathed in flames.

Chapter 38

"—maybe we should—"

"—so glad to see all of—"

"—doctor wouldn't do any—"

"—hurt bad?"

I opened my eyes and bit back a shriek. Sinclair, Marc, Tina, and Garrett were all bending over me. I chased them all back with big arm motions and sat up. I saw at once we were in the hospital.

But had we gotten here in time?

"Where is she?" I managed. Then Sinclair's mouth was on mine, his arms were around me, and I sort of forgot about all the madness of the evening for a minute.

"Wait, wait!" I fended him off and looked around. We were in the right room, I thought. But they all looked alike. "Did it work? Where is she?"

"It's so wonderful to see you're all right, Your Majesty!"

I smiled as I turned to Tina. "When did you two get here?"

"I got home an hour ago," she said, the circles under her eyes even darker than usual. "Marc had just shown up, and then Sinclair called. Um. Why is Antonia a wolf?"

"You wouldn't believe it if I told you."

"Elizabeth did it, right after she destroyed Marjorie. And nearly killed herself for her trouble." Sinclair turned to me—well, really, he turned *on* me, like a wolverine. "Did you not hear me telling you to stay away?" he demanded, shaking me like a cheap Christmas present.

"Oh, stuff it in your socks, Sinclair. Like I was going to leave you in the clutches of the librarian from Hell. What a *bitch*."

"You're sure you're okay?" Marc, being the doctor he was, began to prod my body.

"I—think so." I felt all right. Almost normal. Normal for me, I meant. Gone was the frantic surge of energy I'd feared would consume me.

And from the way they were looking at me, they all knew it. Their expressions were equal parts awe and fear.

But *what* about . . .

"Well, I have to say, I haven't felt this good in quite some time," Garrett said cheerfully. Since he usually spoke in monosyllables, this was going to take some getting used to. "Although I'm not sure what Antonia will say when she's back on two feet tomorrow morning."

"Yeesh, don't give me something new to worry about. By the way, did you notice if the two guests in our house were still there? Are they okay?"

"Jeannie and Lara are fine," Marc said. He was dressed in a shirt studded with big purple flowers, muddy khaki shorts, and sandals. "I made their acquaintance a bit abruptly in the bathroom; but we sorted it out as Tina arrived. After Sinclair called, it was clear the danger was pretty much over, so they opted to stay in the mansion."

"Great. Now that we've accounted for everyone EXCEPT the person we came for, *can someone please tell me where my best friend is!?!*"

This got a couple of them smiling. Which got me steaming even hotter. Finally, Marc piped up. "Well, we got you here, and your boyfriend did what you told him to do. He dumped you right on top of Jessica, who until then was resting comfortably. By then, you weren't in flames anymore—but you were still giving off tons of heat and sweat. Seeing you roll back and forth on top of Jessica in her bed—well, I'll tell you. I almost turned heterosexual."

"But the bed's empty now! Did it work? Is she okay?"

"Better than okay," Tina said, smiling. She was flushed at Marc's description, but she managed to motion to the hallway. "After Detective Berry's initial shock, he saw what we were doing for Jessica and kept you on top of her. Once she was—once you were both okay—well, Jessica and Nick wanted to find some privacy, and we were all in the room, and you still looked like you needed the bed, and so—"

My jaw dropped in appalled outrage. "She's out *getting some?*"

"In a word," Tina began.

"Yeppers," Marc finished.

"Why that—that—"

"They're still somewhere in the hospital," Sinclair gently corrected me.

As if on cue, Jessica and Nick burst into the room (well, burst through the slowly opening door), giggling and leaning on each other. She was still in her wrinkled hospital gown, and his shirt was decidedly untucked from his pants. No socks. No shoes.

"Well, that was—" She saw all of us waiting for her and clammed up.

"Short?" Marc volunteered.

I knew the moment I saw her that it was gone. For good. She looked beautiful.

I stared. We all stared. Finally, Marc cleared his throat and said, "How are you feeling, Jessica?"

Beaming, she pulled away from Nick and spread her arms wide. "I feel *great*. But I'm super-duper hungry. Anybody have a candy bar in their pocket? Or possibly a steak?"

Finally, she turned to me, still grinning like a fool. "Bets, you look like shit. What happened?"

Chapter 39

Sinclair carried me up to bed the moment we got home, which was silly because I could walk perfectly well. I was pretty sure. Actually, given that it was only about 1:00 a.m. I was awfully tired.

The last thing I felt before I conked off was him pulling my engagement ring off my finger. I hope he threw it into the nearest sewer. Boy, was I going to give him a piece of my mind when I . . .

★   ★   ★

$\mathscr{I}$ sat up. The bedside clock said 5:30 p.m. Sinclair was at his desk, scribbling on papers, but looked up and was at my side in half a second.

"Elizabeth—"

"Dead."

"—are you—"

"You are so *dead*."

"—all right?"

"You gave me a *used* engagement ring?" I yelped.

He looked pained as he sat down beside me. "Antique."

"Used."

"As you like. I am very sorry."

I slumped back against the pillows and slapped a hand over my eyes. "You couldn't have known. Friendly helpful Marjorie, right?"

"I thought a ring set with stones that had belonged to a queen would be a fitting gift."

"Zombie. Dead dad. Dead stepmother. Well, the dead stepmother might actually not be so bad . . . but then YOU almost died!"

"I am very sorry."

I removed my hand and looked at him. His fierce

dark gaze was boring into me, and his hands were trembling. "Oh, hey. Like I said. You couldn't have known. You got rid of it, right?"

"I did. I—"

"Never mind. I don't care if I never see the thing again, and I sure don't want to know what you did with it. Also, we're going to Tiffany's to pick out a new one, right?"

"If you wish."

"You look like hell."

"I was . . . terrified for you. I was certain she would kill you. And I was useless. Worse than useless. I could hear what was happening but could not help. I—"

"Come here," I said. "Have I mentioned I missed you like crazy?"

"Not that I recall."

"Well, I have. Missed you like crazy, I mean." I was tugging at his shirt, and buttons were flying all over the place. "Place just isn't the same without you. And hey! Next time the Big Bad lures you out of the house, maybe you could leave a note?"

"Or even text message you," he agreed solemnly. I was frantic to get his clothes off, frantic to touch him, feel him, taste him. I heard cloth tear as I got his shirt off, broke his belt buckle, tore at his pants.

I gripped his hips with my knees and knelt down to have a bite or two. Or three. Oh boy, oh boy, oh *boy*!

"Oh boy," he groaned.

It was so fucking fine to have him in my house, my bed. It was everything I'd missed and then some. It was a dream come true.

(For me as well, my own.)

And oh, it was so good to feel him against me, his hands on me. I pulled at him until we were both sitting up, me still on top, and we kissed hungrily, as if we couldn't get enough air. Or enough of each other. He pushed and I went over . . .

. . . and then I pushed, and I was back on top again.

Mine, I thought.

Yours, he agreed.

I straddled him to get closer, to take him inside of me, and rode him with great delight, staring at the ceiling while his fingers dug into my hip bones. He nipped at my fingers, and I swooped down to kiss him again.

Oh, Sinclair.

Elizabeth. My own, my queen, my dread queen.

Wait a minute. Are we—?

I beg you. Do not destroy the moment with a rude gesture or thought.

But we're—

Yes.

You can—

Yes.

I love you.

Yes. Oh, yes. Right . . .

. . . there.

Chapter 40

Here comes the bride," I hummed, slipping into my shoes. "All dressed in white. (And red.) Here comes the bride, back from the dead. (Again.)"

"That song blows." Jessica leaned over my shoulder to freshen her lipstick with my mirror. "And don't get me started on your singing voice."

"Cured your cancer and all I get is grief."

"Hey, I didn't *make* you cure me. By the way, is it just me or is everyone still *freaked out* about what you did the other night?"

"Yeah, well. I'm not exactly sure what it is I did."

"Neither are Sinclair or Tina. That's why it's driving them nuts."

"Not to mention Michael and the others," Antonia piped up, coming into the dressing room without knocking, as was her habit. "They're gonna walk soft around you for a while. Heh. Oh, and bimbo? Next time you've got two dead guys in coffins and me in a cage, lively and ready to kick ass, let *me* out first! I could have helped you with that rotten monkey Marjorie."

"I'll keep it in mind."

"Least now I know what the fuss is all about," she muttered, waving away Jessica's offer of a mascara wand. "Running around as a wolf is *fun*." She fussed with her lapels and managed only to hopelessly rumple her ruby jacket. "But you know? I haven't had a vision since the one indicating Sinclair shouldn't go to Marjorie's alone. I wonder if I can still see the future."

"Well," I said, feeling uncomfortable, "if you can't, and you miss it, I'm sorry. I didn't—"

"Can it, Betsy. I'm not bitching. Just wondering."

"Will you hold still?" Jessica demanded. Her suit, a twin to Antonia's, was sapphire blue. "You're all rumpled."

"And you're all annoying, but I'm putting up with

that shit, aren't I? I'm here in the middle of monkey rituals, aren't I?"

"Shut up," I said warmly.

Tina rapped on the door, then poked her head inside. "It's almost time, Majesty. My! You're breathtaking."

"It's true," I said modestly. Tina was in the same Vera Wang suit as Jessica and Antonia, except hers was buttercup yellow. With Tina's teeny frame and big dark eyes, and cascades of blond hair, it worked.

Everything worked. It was my day, and everything worked.

I sighed happily and applied more blush. "Hey, did Sinclair talk to you about the new job?"

"What new job?" Jessica asked.

"We need a new librarian," I told my reflection, and grinned. "The last one came down with a slight case of death."

"I have many responsibilities here in the mansion," Tina said. "I will have to consider this very carefully."

"Crissake, when don't you consider everything very carefully?" Antonia yawned and—I wasn't sure how she did this without moving—rumpled her suit jacket again.

"But the chance to get my hands on all those tomes . . ." Tina was practically drooling. "The opportunity for pure research alone makes it a tempting prize."

"Yeah, yeah. Tempting. Betsy, lighten up with the Peach Parfait or you'll be all slutted out."

"Here, let *me.*" Jessica snatched the blusher from my hands and grabbed a tissue with the other hand. She rubbed my cheeks, and for an awful moment I thought she was going to spit on the Kleenex.

"Hmm," Tina said. That was all, just, "Hmm."

"How can you screw up blush?" Jessica was bitching. "You make it look like you're blushing. Then you stop."

"Hmm."

"Will all of you bitches just leave me alone?" I cried.

"The warning cry of the Raptor Bridal Bird," Antonia snickered.

"Look how snotty you got since you found out you are able to turn into a wolf."

"And when your boyfriend remembered how to read. Oh, and that he has a master's in math."

"That's it!" Tina cried, startling all of us into

shutting up. "You never feed, Majesty, compared to us you never feed. So you're always hungry. Always. You think that's how it's supposed to be. For you, hunger is as much a state of the mind as it is of the body. So when Marjorie was killing you, your instinct wasn't to reach with your teeth. It was to *reach with your mind*!"

She was on her feet, screeching that last.

Antonia stared. I stared. Jessica corrected my blush.

"Um. Excuse me," she muttered, smoothing her skirt.

My mom poked her head in the room. "Are you ready?"

"Yeah," Antonia replied.

"I think she was talking to me," I said.

"Oh, yeah, like it's all about you."

"Today it is. Let's do it!"

ou may kiss the bride," Judge Summit informed us, and Sinclair was too glad to comply. He'd done a remarkable job of concealing his boredom during the brief ceremony, though his dark eyes had gleamed at the sight of me in my gown.

The guests (all the usual suspects, plus the Wynd-hams) clapped politely and, as we went back down the aisle, tossed little paper hearts instead of rice.

"They're throwing paper hearts? At vampires?" Sinclair bitched.

"Oh, hush up and try to enjoy the moment."

But why didn't you tell me you thought there'd be a problem with Sinclair going to see Mar-jorie?" I asked while the others devoured the choco-late cake (with raspberry filling!) and I tried not to drool. Too bad solid food made me barf.

"She dealt with the problem directly," Michael ex-plained. "She teamed up with the alpha male and tried to support him. Going to you would have been . . ."

"Useless?" I offered.

"Unnecessary," Antonia corrected me, but her cheeks were red. She had underestimated how much I could help, and who could blame her? I wouldn't have thought I could do much, either.

At least not until today.

"Culture clash," Derik said cheerfully, wolfing down his second slice of cake. "Antonia has spent too much time with you vampires. A true werewolf would have sought to put together the largest pack possible."

"Yeah, well, a true werewolf can kiss my ass," Antonia offered.

"You are a true werewolf," Michael pointed out. "You always have been."

"Come on, pack leader. Don't deny there'll be some at home who will finally decide I'm actually worthy of the secret handshake."

Michael said nothing, but Derik broke the tension by showering Antonia in cake crumbs.

"Anyway," Tina put in, batting a few wayward crumbs out of her hair, "everything worked out fine that day, thanks to Her Majesty. Now people will know better than to ask you, Eric, when they need help." She delivered this last line with a nasty, but still friendly, smile.

"I will pretend my feelings aren't lacerated," Sinclair said dryly. His hand was resting on my shoulder. In fact, since I'd rescued him, he was always touching me somewhere or other. Not that I minded in the slightest. I was also loving the fact that we were spending most of our evenings trying to hurt each other during lovemaking.

I glanced down at my new rings. Traditional wedding band and engagement ring. Platinum bands (Sinclair had the twin), one carat diamond setting. *Not* used. *Not* cursed.

And Sinclair had taken the news that he was BabyJon's new daddy with remarkable calm. I suspected he still felt tremendous guilt over giving me the cursed ring in the first place. So it was only fair that he would help me raise this kid for the next seventeen or eighteen years.

"So where are you guys off to?" Laura asked. We'd made up just before the wedding, and she had apologized. I'd told her that dear old Mom had dropped by from Hell, and she'd been horrified. She'd suited up in her Vera Wang (emerald green, the color of her eyes when she was eeeeevil). We were fine again. For now.

"New York City," Sinclair replied. The one aspect of the wedding he'd actually taken an interest in was planning the honeymoon. "And I thank you for taking the baby while we're gone."

"Oh, it's my pleasure," Laura gushed.

"We're leaving him behind?" I cried. "But he'll miss us! Me."

"Sorry, my wife. On that I draw the line. Babies and honeymoons do not mix."

"Fascist," I muttered, but I didn't put any real heat into it. In three days I'd gone from lonely and frightened to surrounded by friends, family, and new allies. And Jessica was all better! "You wait until later."

"I dream of later," he murmured back.

I laughed and squeezed his hand. Poor guy, he was holding up pretty well under all the nuttiness. Werewolves, a queen with mondo weird new powers, his privacy shattered by hordes, all who wanted to talk to me. Don't even get me started on BabyJon. So I knew he was looking forward to ditching the group as much as I was, but he didn't know what I'd gotten him for a wedding gift.

Spray-on gourmet flavors. I had bought him Turkey, Gravy, Raspberry, Hash Browns, and Baked Alaska.

I could hardly wait to squirt them all over him. And I'd never been to the Big Apple. I planned to take a great big bite.

"—my own."

"What?"

"I said, come along for a moment, my own. I have something to show you . . . upstairs."

I glanced at our guests. They had broken off into small groups and were chatting about this and that.

"Race you," I whispered, and chased him all the way to our bedroom.